DUSTY WAGONS

DUSTY WAGONS

Matt Stuart

Chivers Press • G.K. Hall & Co.
Bath, Avon, England   Thorndike, Maine USA

This Large Print edition is published by Chivers Press, England, and by G.K. Hall & Co., USA.

Published in 1995 in the U.K. by arrangement with the author c/o the Golden West Literary Agency.

Published in 1995 in the U.S. by arrangement with the Golden West Literary Agency.

U.K. Hardcover ISBN 0–7451–2559–X (Chivers Large Print)
U.S. Softcover   ISBN 0–7838–1149–7 (Nightingale Collection
                                     Edition)

An earlier version of this novel was serialized in *Ranch Romances*.

The text of this Large Print edition is unabridged.
Other aspects of the book may vary from the original edition.

Set in 16 pt. New Times Roman.

Printed in Great Britain on acid-free paper.

British Library Cataloguing in Publication Data available

Library of Congress Cataloging-in-Publication Data

Stuart, Matt, 1895–
    Dusty wagons / by Matt Stuart.
      p.   cm.
    ISBN 0–7838–1149–7 (lg. print : lsc)
    1. Large type books.   I. Title.
[PS3515.O4448D87   1995]
813'.52—dc20
                                                95–6688

CONTENTS

CONTENTS

DUSTY WAGONS

CHAPTER ONE

WAGON MAN

Under a velvet sky pierced with a million cool, white stars, Gene Cuyler came down from the north across the Vaca Plains along the old Fort Rutledge road. With close to two hundred dusty miles put behind them since leaving Iron Springs, both rider and horse knew the weight of weariness, and the lights of the town of Capell, winking out of the night ahead, brought welcome promise of food and rest.

Across these level plains the lights had been in view for the past two hours and, as was sometimes the way with lights at night, never seemed to get any closer, always dancing way out there in the dark, still distance, elusive and tantalizing. Cuyler, from the depths of his hunger and saddle fatigue, eyed them almost resentfully.

Now another glow took place, a little to one side of the clustered lights of the town, a glow that became suddenly a bursting spread of flame, rippling and snapping upward. It was not large enough to be a building of any size, yet it was too definitely shaped to be a mere bonfire. It was something to stir Cuyler out of the stoic mechanics of long riding so now he shifted in his saddle and built a smoke while he

1

pondered the significance of that sudden flame.

Abruptly his senses registered another break in the night's vast and bland indifference. This time it was sound. He twisted still further in the saddle, tipped his head and listened. Faint at the moment but climbing rapidly in volume was the rolling tattoo of racing hoofs, storming up from behind.

Freshly built cigarette between his lips, Cuyler had been about to strike a match. Now he held back on this and instead reined his horse off the road. For some time along the plain he had been passing towering valley oak trees, mounded blots of gloom in the wider dark. One such stood not far off and Cuyler rode into the protective shadow of it, halting there while he laid a quickening alertness along the back trail.

The approaching hoofs were now a solid rushing. Closebunched, the riders exploded past, a full half dozen of them, leaving the night heavy with the dry, parched odor of churned-up dust and the ranker, acrid smell of sweating horseflesh. Cuyler waited where he was for a full five minutes, then lighted his cigarette, sought the road again and rode on.

Within another half mile the lights of Capell were no longer elusive and taunting, disembodied flecks in the night. They stilled and grew brighter, took on the solid square and rectangular shapes of open doors and unshuttered windows; the whole town took on

2

bulk and form under the stars. Now, also, there lifted the voice of the town and there was a sullen, threatening note in it, the growling clamor of angry men.

Gene Cuyler reined in, let a keening speculation run out ahead of him. His glance swung to where that sudden flame had lifted through the dark and he could make out now exactly what it was that the fire was consuming. The knowledge sent a tautness through him and an anger that brought his big shoulders swinging forward and thinned his lips across his teeth.

It was a wagon that was burning, a big, gaunt freight wagon. It was far gone. The sides and bed had burned through and were collapsing. The reach was a long line of ruddy flame between front and rear axles, and the wooden portions of these were also ablaze. Every spoke was outlined in flickering crimson, every felloe a circle of red, every hub a solid ball of the same consuming color.

Even as Cuyler watched, the off rear wheel collapsed. In swift succession the other three wheels did the same. Sparks shot upward, a thousand lurid fireflies winging against the stars. The crackle of flames fell to a settled, satisfied mutter.

Now above the rumble of the town lifted a sudden, shrill yipping, the taunting yell of saddlemen on the loose. Hoofs pounded and several mounted figures streamed past the

3

outer lights of the town, to race round and around the fading mound of flame that had been a freight wagon.

Wild, flitting figures they were, outlined against the red glow. Cuyler, watching, knew a start of surprise. Beyond question, the rider in the lead was a girl, a lithe riding fury with a banner of yellow hair streaming out behind her. As the riders sped back into town again the girl's triumphant cry lifted clear above the deeper-toned yells of her male companions.

A harshness built up in Cuyler's eyes, turning them bleak and frosty. Apparently the word he had picked up as far away as Iron Springs about the tides of feeling flowing over the Vaca Plains and around this town of Capell had not been exaggerated. About to rein away, Cuyler stopped again. Out there, a little way in the night, someone was crying and a deep voice trying to comfort, a sound and solid voice with a touch of brogue in it.

'Now, now, Mary—we'll not be after wastin' any more tears over a lost cause. Sure, and it was a good wagon, an honest Merivale wagon, with none better. But we'll get another and when we do, if any of those spur-wearing sons of Satan come ridin' fancy and wild to burn it, then it'll be Mike Kenna himself who'll fill their hides so full of buckshot they'll—whist! Yonder's one of them now, viewing his dirty work and proud of it, no doubt!'

Cuyler saw the pair of them, just touched by

4

the reach of the dying, ruddy light of the fire. A stocky, bearded man, with a comforting arm about a figure in calico. The man spoke again, his words and his glance pointing at Cuyler.

'Ay! No doubt it's proud that you are, cowboy, now that you've put Mike Kenna and his good wife afoot, with no other means of earnin' an honest living. Yet it's a pride which will not last. You'll yet be sorry for what you've done this night to us, and to others of the freighting trade.'

Cuyler answered gravely. 'You've got me wrong, friend. I'm no cow hand and I had no part in burning your wagon. I'm a stranger here, just arrived. I'm sorry about your misfortune.'

Again Cuyler started to rein away, but now once more that little group of riders came bursting out of town, to race a circle about the dying flames of the wagon. Still leading them was the girl with the pale, wild-flying hair.

Now another mounted figure came up to the fading light, to lift a ringing call. Another girl and, despite the exasperation in it, her voice was round and full and clear with music.

'Candy! Candy Loftus! Uncle Ben says you're to stop this wild, crazy racing around and come over to the store with me. Candy—do you hear?'

If the girl with the pale, streaming hair heard, she paid no attention, for now, with her male companions, she had pulled to a halt in a

5

half circle about Mike Kenna and his wife and one of the riders spoke harshly.

'You won't be told again, Mike Kenna. You and your wife get down to the mule corrals and stay there, along with the rest of your kind. For in the mornin' you're all heading back to Sycamore, where you'll stay if you know what's good for you. We're not lettin' any of you stick around Capell. Get that, Kenna—not any of you! Now amble on down to the corrals—and hurry up!'

'We'll go, the good wife and I,' retorted Mike Kenna with a fine, calm dignity. 'Yet we'll not be hurried by such as you, Blaze Doan. All the belongings of Mary and me were in that wagon, little things that were near and dear to us. You burned them, along with our wagon. Now you would deny us the right to spend a quiet moment by the ashes of what was almost a home to us. A low business—a mighty low business.'

Another of the riders moved his horse slightly ahead. 'I'm tired of palaver and talk,' he growled. 'Maybe a little touch of leather will put some life and action into you, Kenna.' The speaker flicked the lash of his quirt restlessly.

Mike Kenna seemed to grow taller, straighter. 'You touch Mary or me with that quirt, Huntoon—and I'll have your life, if it be the last thing I ever do on this earth.'

The rider laughed jeeringly, swung the quirt high.

6

Gene Cuyler sent his horse lunging forward and his voice cut across the night like cold acid.

'Drop that quirt!'

When Cuyler set his horse up, he and the animal formed a barrier between the Kennas and the threat of the lash. Cuyler's abrupt move into the scene held the mounted group for a moment of poised surprise. Then the rider with the quirt leaned forward.

'Who are you? What outfit d'you ride for?'

'None,' was the brittle answer. 'Just so you'll remember, the name is Cuyler—Gene Cuyler. Put that quirt away and back up. You and your kind have done these good people enough dirt for one night. Touch either of them with that quirt and I'll use the butt end of it on that thick skull of yours. You heard me. Back up!' In the saddle, Cuyler loomed a tall, flat shape against the stars.

The yellow-haired girl spoke. 'He needs a lesson himself, Cass. Give it to him!'

Down across the Vaca Plains, Cass Huntoon had never been recognized for any mental brilliance, but he did have a reputation as a rough-and-tumble fighter. So now, encouraged by the girl, he swung his quirt high, standing in his stirrups to get his full weight and strength into the blow.

'You asked for it, Mister Gene Cuyler. Here it is!'

Cuyler's move was explosive. He gigged his horse sharply, leaning far forward and lifting

7

his mount ahead in a sharp lunge that brought him up on Huntoon's left side. The down whipping lash, hissing as it fell, scraped the back of Cuyler's shirt and cracked like a pistol shot across the cantle of his saddle.

Came the sound of another blow, deeper and fleshier than the other as Cuyler, rolling his shoulder to get power into the punch, smashed his right fist into Huntoon's face, shaking the fellow up, hurting and dazing him. Before he could recover, Cuyler tore the quirt from his grip and clubbed him savagely with the loaded butt. Cass Huntoon toppled and slithered soddenly from his saddle.

Gene Cuyler kneed his horse around and now he had the quirt in one hand and a gun in the other. He urged his horse ahead, straight at the yellow-haired girl and he lashed at her with words.

'Candy—the other one called you. It should have been poison. Speaking of a lesson being needed, how about one for yourself? I'd say you had one coming, and long overdue. As long as you're so fond of the other guy testing a quirt lash, maybe a little bite of the same will teach you a lesson. Candy! What a laugh!'

The quirt sang as Cuyler slashed empty air with it.

The girl dragged her horse back. 'You—you wouldn't dare!'

'Now wouldn't I!' mocked Cuyler. 'You'd be surprised. As for your friends who call

8

themselves men, if any of them want a slug where it'll do the most good, all they have to do is ask for it. Just so you'll get everything straight, I'll tell you what I am. I'm a wagon man, and I don't stand around and see other wagon folk bullied or kicked around by such as you and yours. Tough is what you fancy yourselves, maybe? Well, let's see how tough you brave buckaroos are. Now is a good time to demonstrate. No—you don't want any of such right now? Then break it up! Get the hell out of here before somebody really gets hurt!'

Cuyler's scathing words fell like thrown projectiles. There was a cold and wicked anger welling out of him like a thrusting wall. The group broke and gave back, all except the yellow-haired girl. She seemed unable to move. Her face was white in the starlight, a frightened face.

Cuyler laughed harshly. 'Scared plumb to death. Just a wild-riding little fake. Just a yellow-haired little four-flusher and bully. A minute ago a tough, arrogant little fool. Now scared witless, but still a fool!'

A horse came pushing in from the side, the other girl in this saddle. She put her mount and herself between Cuyler and the shrinking object of his scathing words. She sat straight and proud in her saddle. Under the stars her bared head seemed raven black.

'You'll not touch her,' she said. 'She's just a heedless child.'

9

'She's a spoiled, silly little brat,' rapped Cuyler. 'But you're right—I won't touch her. She's not worth it.'

The dark-haired one turned in her saddle and said, 'Come on, Candy.'

This time there was no argument. Candy rode away with her, still and subdued.

The male riders were uneasy, undecided. Then the voice of Blaze Doan lifted.

'You got the jump out here, mister. But you'll be wise to cut away from this town and keep on traveling.'

'I'll be ridin' right down the middle of your damn town in a couple of minutes,' shot back Cuyler. 'And let's see you bully boys try and stop me! Or, if you want, you can cut your wolf loose right here and now. Only, I don't think it's wolf. I think it's mainly coyote.'

He waited for them to make their play, one way or the other. They shifted about, muttering, but finally reined away and followed the two girls back into town.

Cuyler dismounted, got Cass Huntoon's gun and tossed it far out into the dark. Then, leading his horse, he strode over to Mike and Mary Kenna, who had been silent and somewhat awed witnesses to the whole affair.

'A mighty tough break, friend, to lose your wagon like that,' said Cuyler. 'But you haven't lost your means of making a living. For you showed a level head and a good brand of nerve. I'm going to need both in my business.'

10

Mike Kenna looked at him searchingly. 'I heard the word you gave them that you were a wagon man. Yet you sit a saddle like you were born to it.'

Cuyler shrugged. 'I can get around quicker in a saddle. Here it is, short and sweet. I'm going to set up a freight line running out of Capell and down to Sycamore on the other side of the Brushy Hills. I've got a pretty good string of wagons coming in. I aim to get more and I'll need men to drive them for me. Think about that. I'll see you later, down at the corrals.'

Kenna drew a deep breath. 'You made them crawl this time, Gene Cuyler. But there are more and tougher ones than Blaze Doan and Cass Huntoon and that spoiled, silly girl, Candy Loftus. I'm glad you did not strike her with that quirt.'

Cuyler barked a terse laugh. 'Never meant to, but she didn't know that. Now you and the missus better be gettin' along. Huntoon shows signs of gettin' his wits back and he may turn ugly. I'll see you later.'

This town of Capell was of fair size, a town that had been there a long time, buildings weathered but solid with permanence. The single street, running almost due north and south, lay wide and dusty white under the stars except where several big oaks loomed, to throw dark blots of wide shadow. Hitch rails sagged along both sides of the street and between them

11

and the buildings ran a foot-high sidewalk of warped and splintery boards.

The uproar had quieted, but plenty of men were around, standing in little groups or moving restlessly back and forth, wary shadows drifting past the flares of yellow light which reached out from door and window. Tension and the poised threat of further violence still lay across the night and Gene Cuyler had the feeling that any little thing might break matters wide open again.

With the first rush of bleak anger now running out of him, Cuyler knew that he wasn't showing the best of judgment in pacing his horse slowly down the center of this wide, tense street. But he had made his brag to Blaze Doan and those other riders so now he had to go through with it.

That Doan had spread the word was quite apparent. Cuyler could feel the impact of many eyes; and the cold, prickling alertness running up and down his spine told him of the thought behind this scrutiny. Yet no one spoke or made an attempt at stopping him until he came even with a big, square, two-story building with many windows and a wide double door through which yellow light poured to flood a portion of the veranda. A hotel.

Figures were drifting up and down that veranda and, even as Cuyler watched, two feminine figures went through the open door. In the light, one head shone fair, the other

12

raven black.

Now, moving out into the street came a dark group of men and a harsh voice lashed.

'Far enough, mister. You can stop right there!'

Cuyler reined in, crossed his hands on his saddle horn and leaned his big shoulders slightly forward. His voice went out in a cool, dry drawl.

'I've stopped. Where do we go from here?'

'You a wagon man?' came the demand.

'I'm a wagon man.'

'Then you can pick any direction that takes your fancy. But go, and keep on going. Don't come back!'

'No!' Cuyler spoke the word almost gently. 'I recognize the right of no man to tell me where I must go or where I can or can't stop. I've come a long way to get to Capell. I'm staying here.'

A note of grudging admiration was in the voice which lifted at him again.

'Too bad you're a wagon man. You got nerve enough to be something better.'

'Nerve enough to kick peaceful folks around and burn their wagons maybe?' Cuyler's tone was even, but the sarcasm in it dry and biting.

'That deal is our business and none of yours,' came the sharp reply. 'You made your brag about ridin' down the middle of this street. All right, you've made the brag good, if that gives you any satisfaction. Now you'd

13

better start using common sense, for you're right up against the end of the string. Head out and keep on going. That is the final word of Ben Loftus and you'd better believe I mean it!'

Gene Cuyler let his right hand drop to where the bulk of his holstered gun lay against his thigh.

'No!' he said once more.

Cried Ben Loftus, almost regretfully, 'You damned, stubborn fool! I hoped to avoid the extreme. But it looks like you won't learn any other way. Spread out, boys!'

The shadowy group stirred, but went swiftly still again as a deep, rolling voice reached out from the blackness under one of the oaks on the far side of the street, directly across from the hotel.

'Easy does it, Loftus! This is Jim Nickerson—and not alone. We got here too late to help Mike Kenna and the other wagon men, but we're not too late to side that fellow you're trying to run a shindy on now. Cut it fine, Loftus—cut it fine!'

The effect on the group facing Cuyler was marked and immediate. They swung to face the threat in the blackness under the oak, then were still, while Ben Loftus gave his reply.

'Nickerson! Out from behind your damned barbed wire at last, eh? I can put up the cry and you'll never get behind it again with a sound hide.'

'Take that double for yourself,' rumbled

14

Nickerson. 'I'm looking right down your throat, Loftus, over a sawed-off shotgun. If you want to see blood in the dust of this street, yours will be the first to run. Make your cry a real good war whoop, for it will be your last. You cowmen have been itching for this. Now you can have it. Put up or shut up!'

That booming, rolling challenge reached far. It reached to the interior of the hotel apparently, for now, from that open door a raven-haired figure came running, her voice speeding out ahead.

'Uncle Ben—stop this thing! Stop it, now! It has gone far enough.'

She ran right in among the dark blot of men blocking the street. Ben Loftus challenged her angrily.

'You, Paula—get along back into the hotel with Candy. This is no place or business for a girl. You hear me? Get back inside!'

'No! No, I won't. I have something to say about what J L riders should do. They are not to start any more trouble. It is my right, my authority to order them to quit this wild business and get back to the ranch. And I'm giving them that order, now! You all hear me? Get out of town and back to the ranch!'

'You crazy girl!' raged Loftus. 'If shooting starts you might—!'

'If shooting starts it will be your fault. And, uncle or no uncle, I'll hold you responsible.'

'That's telling the pig-headed old fool, Paula

15

Juilliard,' boomed Jim Nickerson. 'You got more common sense and justice in that pretty head of yours than him and all his cowmen friends.'

In his saddle, Gene Cuyler relaxed. There would be, he knew now, no shooting. And, as the center of argument, it would be wise to get out of sight. He reined his horse over to the black shadow of the oak tree.

'That's smart, friend,' murmured Jim Nickerson. 'Leaves Ben Loftus punching and cussing at an empty street. That niece of his has taken the wind right out of his sails. He's beginning to feel foolish. This will end up a quiet night, after all. I heard you say you were a wagon man. Where are your wagons?'

'Coming,' replied Cuyler briefly. 'Down along the Fort Rutledge road, about two days back. Six double outfits. Merivales with back actions. I hear there is wheat to be hauled in this country?'

'You heard right. Wheat and more wheat. Barns full of it and another big crop coming along. The job of hauling that wheat across the Brushy Hills and down to Sycamore, where the river boats come up, is all yours if you can stick it. What you saw happen tonight is only a mild sample of the trouble that'll be in your trail. But if you can stick it, you can haul wheat.'

'I'll stick it,' said Cuyler. 'I'll haul wheat. That's what I came here for. Yeah, I'll haul wheat!'

16

CHAPTER TWO

DIGGING IN

It was at Iron Springs, a hundred and fifty miles beyond old Fort Rutledge, that Gene Cuyler had been operating his freight line when he first heard of the explosive condition building up on the Vaca Plains. Cuyler's wagons had been hauling for the mines at Iron Springs, but the mines were showing signs of playing out and Cuyler had known for some time that eventually he would have to pull out and look for new fields of business.

Down on the Vaca Plains, so the word had it, there was wheat to be hauled, endless tons of it. But the word also said that there was trouble on the Vaca Plains between cattlemen and the wheat farmers, over the oldest point of conflict in the West. Land. Open Range.

Vast acreage of the plains was government land which for years the cattlemen had utilized as their own. Until now that the wheat farmer had moved in, filed on the land, run his fences, broken the sod and planted his wheat.

It had been battle from the first, but the wheat farmer, coming on in numbers and knowing his rights, had stuck it out, dogged and stubborn and determined. Unable to stop the wheat farmer by other means short of an

17

outright bloody battle to the death, the cattle interests had begun trying other and less awesome tactics.

They had begun putting the pressure on the little band of one- and two-wagon freighters who had been hauling the wheat from the Vaca Plains down across the hills to the head of navigation on the Sarco River. It was the cattlemen's idea that if they could break up the initial transport of the wheat, they would leave the farmers without access to a market, in which case the latter, broke and discouraged, would give up altogether.

These were the sorts of stories to reach Gene Cuyler at Iron Springs and, because he was young and because there was something in his make-up that rose instinctively to challenge the difficult and dangerous, he had decided to move in on a situation which older and more conservative judgments would have gone to considerable lengths to avoid. He had determined to take his wagons down to the Vaca Plains and dare the wrath of the cattle interests.

Affecting this decision was also a strain of shrewd, hard-headed business judgment. For, reasoned Cuyler, if he should move in and stick, where other men weakened and left, he would establish a permanent and lasting business, dig his roots deep, and be set for all the future years. What matter that it was a gamble in which he might find disaster even

18

more surely than he would find success? All life was a gamble, and no man had ever won big rewards without taking some chances.

That the stories of conditions on the Vaca Plains had in no way been exaggerated, Cuyler had full evidence. Violence had marched across the town of Capell this night. Cuyler had seen a freight wagon burned. He had heard and taken threats. At the wagon camp on the southern outskirts of town was a group of freighters, beaten, clubbed, discouraged. But there was still wheat to be hauled, barns full of it, so Jim Nickerson had told him.

Thinking of all these things as he went, Cuyler circled to the southern edge of town, moving on foot, leading his weary horse. At the wagon camp a few fires flickered, small and discouraged, reflecting the mood of the wagon men themselves.

There was, mused Cuyler, one single big reason why such a group of men would never successfully stand up against the weight of the cattlemen. The cattlemen were organized, while these wagon men were not.

Cuyler knew his one-wagon freighters. They were stubbornly independent, each one dead set on paddling his own canoe in his own way, intolerant of the other fellow's ideas, staunch to his own. Operating singly, hauling how they pleased and when they pleased, there was no strength in them beyond that of one man and one outfit at a time. Capitalizing on this, the cattlemen were certain to whip them, every time out.

About the campfires squatted sullen, dispirited men. Nearly all of them showed signs of recent combat. Some had bandages about clubbed heads. One or two had an arm in a sling. A few women were in evidence, some in jeans and hickory shirts, others in calico. They were brewing coffee, cooking food, tending the hurts of their men.

As Cuyler moved past the different fires, sullen glances followed him. Abruptly a burly skinner jumped up and his voice rang out, thick and hoarse.

'They can beat us over the head, they can break our bones and burn our wagons. But damn me if they can send one of their spies to prowl our camp. Get out, you—or I'll brain you with this whiffletree!'

He came at Cuyler, backed by a growl of approval from several others. Cuyler squared around, facing him.

'Easy, friend—easy! You got me wrong. I'm not a cowman. I'm one of your kind, a wagon man.'

'You got spurs on and there's the smell of saddle leather all through you,' charged the skinner. 'You're not fooling me. You're a damned spy!'

Other men, simmering, sullen hate breaking loose in them, were up and closing in. One of them encouraged, 'Go ahead, Hitch. Smash

20

him. Knock his skull in!'

Cuyler spread his feet, rocked forward a trifle, his big shoulders solid and set.

'Go slow!' he warned, both his tone and his eyes turning frosty. 'I tell you I'm a wagon man and I come as a friend. But nobody takes a cut at me with a club. That means—nobody!' He slapped a hand sharply against the butt of his gun.

This slowed them. An older man spoke up. 'I've been rolling a wagon for nearly twenty years, all over this part of California. Yet I never laid eyes on you in a wagon camp before.'

'California,' rapped Cuyler, 'is a big state. I'm from up north. The Iron Springs country. Before you gents push your luck too far, I suggest you call Mike Kenna. He'll put you right as to which side I'm on.'

They lifted a call and an answer came from one of the more distant fires. Presently Mike Kenna plodded up. The skinner with the whiffletree demanded, 'You know this guy, Mike? He asked for you. We think he's a damned cow hand spy.'

Cuyler said, 'Ask Mike who clubbed Cass Huntoon with his own quirt butt.'

'Of course,' nodded Kenna. 'You're wrong, Hitch Gower. I vouch for this man. I'm glad of the chance to shake his hand and thank him for taking the part of my Mary and me.'

Cuyler smiled. 'I didn't come looking for

21

thanks, Mike. I came to have that talk with you.'

Kenna jerked his head. 'Over at my fire.'

Mary Kenna was there. Her dark eyes were grave, a little sad, but she gave Cuyler a welcoming smile and did not miss his glance at simmering coffee pot and sizzling frying pan. Quietly she set out another plate and cup on the square of tarpaulin spread beside the fire.

'It is frugal fare,' she said. 'There was little we were able to save from our wagon fire.'

'It is honest fare and you are good to include me, ma'am,' answered Cuyler.

While they ate, Cuyler outlined his plans to Kenna. 'I've had a talk with Nickerson,' he ended. 'He said I could keep a good dozen double-wagon outfits rolling all summer and still not run short of wheat to haul, especially with a fine new crop coming along.'

Mike Kenna nodded emphatically. 'Nickerson did not lie. For I've seen it with my own eyes. Sacked wheat stuffing big barn warehouses to the rafters. Ay, there's plenty of wheat.'

'But right now I haven't got a dozen double-wagon outfits,' said Cuyler. 'I got only six, and I want more. You and the others—are you sticking or quitting, Mike?'

'For myself I am not sure,' answered Mike slowly. 'I would need a new wagon. And with Ben Loftus and Joe Justin and Teede Hunnewell growing meaner by the hour and

22

spreading their violence toward wagon men more and more—well, I've got to be thinkin' of Mary's welfare.'

'And the others?'

Kenna shrugged. 'From the talk I've heard, some will quit. The rest are heading for Sycamore in the morning, through with the Vaca Plains for good, but hoping to pick up a job or two along the Sarco River. Why do you ask this?'

'Because I'd like to hire you on to work for me, Mike. And because I'd like to buy up the outfits of those who are aiming to quit the game entirely. Will you come in with me, Mike?'

'You have known me but an hour or two,' said Kenna. 'Yet you would offer me this job?'

'A man,' said Cuyler quietly, 'is a good man, whether you know him but an hour or a lifetime.'

What with the loss of his own wagon and the sight and company of whipped men all about him, Mike Kenna's eyes had been dull and spiritless. Now a gleam came into them.

'You're usin' some strong bait, lad,' he admitted. 'I can see that it is in you to fight such as Loftus and Justin and Hunnewell to a finish, and I would like a bit of that myself. Yet, I must think of Mary.'

Mrs. Kenna, until now a silent listener, lifted her head.

'If you are thinking of me, Mike Kenna—

23

you will say yes. It's a chance for you to start over again in the trade you love and the only one at which you could ever be happy. Rolling wagons, mules sneezing in the dust, the song of the yoke bells. It's your life, Mike—and mine too, for that matter. So you will take this job.'

Mike Kenna laughed softly. 'There it is, lad. Mary has decided for us. I'll work for you.'

'Keno!' exclaimed Cuyler. 'You start this very night. Visit around. Find out which ones will sell their outfits. You'll know the worth of the wagons and mules. Dicker for six or eight of the best. You can promise spot cash. I'll have it for them in the morning. And any others who are good men and want to work for me, will be welcomed. You'll do that, Mike?'

Mike stood up, filled his chest, stretched his arms. 'Ay, I'll do it. Mary lass, look up. There is star shine again. For a time this night I couldn't get my eyes high enough to see the stars. But I can now—and they are shining.'

'One other thing,' said Cuyler. 'These corrals and feed sheds, Mike—and that windmill I hear, creaking over yonder—who owns them and the ground they stand on?'

'That I do not know, lad,' answered Kenna. 'Before this town was ever here, there was an old Spanish rancho on this spot. In the morning you'll be able to see some of the old adobe buildings still standing. I've heard it said the first corrals were part of that rancho. When the wagon men first came into this country they

24

made use of the corrals and there was no objection. Others then followed suit. The corrals have been rebuilt and repaired by wagon men and, needing steady water, they chipped in, bought a windmill and set it up over the old rancho well. I've never known our use of it to be questioned.'

'That's fine,' nodded Cuyler. 'It makes the setup sound. Mike, I'll see you in the morning.' He bent a quick, flashing smile on Mrs. Kenna. 'Thank you for feeding me, ma'am.'

He unsaddled his weary horse, turned it into the big corral where mules rested and fed in the starlight, shouldered his saddle bags and headed back up town. Capell lay completely quiet now, and most of the saddle stock that had lined the hitch rails earlier in the evening was gone.

Cuyler went into the hotel and over to the yellowed, battered register. Only two men were in sight. They sat at a small table, playing chess. Even as Cuyler came in, one of them moved his queen and said, 'Checkmate!'

The other player stared at the board for a moment, ran a hand through thinning, sandy hair and swore softly.

'Damn you, Pierce! That's the same slickery trap I walked into last time.'

The speaker got up and came over to the desk as Cuyler signed the register in a bold, strong hand.

'Just for the night?' he asked.

'By the month,' Cuyler told him. 'I'll be a regular.'

'Take Number Eleven,' said the hotelkeeper. 'What with drifters and all, I generally ask payment in advance.'

'That's all right,' nodded Cuyler. 'How much?'

The hotelkeeper named the amount and Cuyler paid. Then he said, 'There's a bank in this town. I'd like to meet the owner of it. Maybe you could tell me where I might find him at this time of night?'

'Sure,' said the hotelkeeper, glancing at the register. 'You won't have to look far. That's him yonder. He just gave me another scalping at chess. Shake hands with him. Pierce Pomeroy. Pierce, this is Gene Cuyler.'

Pierce Pomeroy was a slim, precise man, rather handsome in a coldly immaculate way. His hair was thick and black, though graying slightly at the temples. His black eyes were shrewd and sharp and a perfect mask for his thoughts. His hand grip was firm and dry.

'Glad to know you, Cuyler,' he said. 'What can I do for you?'

'I hate to ask any man to talk business, after hours,' said Cuyler. 'But—'

'Come up to my room,' said Pomeroy briskly.

He brought out glasses and a bottle of very good bourbon whiskey and he nodded approvingly as Cuyler took one short one and

26

then refused any more.

'What is this business you want to talk about?' asked Pomeroy.

Cuyler grinned wryly. 'The usual one when a man comes to a banker. Money. Here's the proposition.'

Cuyler explained what he had in mind, the buying up of several outfits from the wagon men who were discouraged and ready to quit. He told of the six double-wagon outfits of his own that were on their way in.

'I've Nickerson's word for it that I can keep twice that many outfits busy. So I want these other outfits. The present owners will want spot cash. I haven't got enough on hand. So, I want to negotiate a loan.'

Pomeroy had lighted a perfecto. Now he rolled this back and forth between his lips, squinting his eyes against the smoke. 'What,' he asked, 'would you offer as collateral?'

'A chattel mortgage on the outfits.'

'Not enough,' said Pomeroy. 'Not enough in view of the present trouble between the cattlemen and you wagon men. Mules can be killed, wagons wrecked or burned.'

'I see your point,' admitted Cuyler, 'and saw the objection coming. But I got to have that money. And I might add that anyone trying to kill my mules or burn my wagons will find they've bitten off a pretty tough mouthful.' There was a grimness about his mouth as he said this.

He could feel Pomeroy studying him, weighing him, measuring him. But he could not get behind Pomeroy's black eyes. The banker asked bluntly, 'What makes you think you could make a winning fight of it against the cattle interests where all the other wagon men have failed? You admit they're whipped, discouraged, and pulling out.'

'I know your little one-hitch teamster,' Cuyler said. 'He's the most independent hombre on earth—too independent some times for his own good. He goes his own way in his own time and does as he damn well pleases. Which is all well and good, except when a ruckus like the present one is going on. Then his own independence is what licks him—he tries to fight alone. My own idea is different. My wagons will roll as a unit, work as a unit and fight as a unit, all under single leadership according to a single plan. We'll be a plenty tough nut to crack, if anybody comes hunting trouble.'

Pomeroy nodded and observed, 'I can see where the big weakness among those other wagon men has always been the fact that they wouldn't work together.' He puffed at his cigar and now his black eyes were narrowed, staring into space. Obviously he was running the proposition over in his mind, calculating chances for success, weighing the penalties of failure. Cuyler waited, spinning a cigarette into shape and thinking that as bankers went, this fellow Pomeroy was as shrewd as they came.

'You're a stranger to me,' said Pomeroy abruptly. 'I've known you about fifteen minutes. You say you've got six double-wagon outfits coming in. I don't *know* that you have. For all I know you could be lying about that.'

A dark flush ran up Gene Cuyler's jaw. He picked up his hat and started for the door. 'Reckon you and me can't do business after all,' he said curtly.

'Sit down—sit down!' murmured Pomeroy, a ghost of a smile touching his lips. 'I merely said you could be lying, not that you were. Remember, I've a right to weigh all angles of this deal. Put it that I was thinking out loud. Come on, sit down and have another drink.'

Cuyler slowly resumed his seat, but shook his head at the proffered bottle. The quick frost in his eyes faded slowly.

'You know, Cuyler,' went on Pomeroy, 'in making a loan we bankers have a common yardstick to guide us. It is known as the 'Three C's—character, collateral, capacity. I've been using that yardstick on you. Judging from how you've handled yourself since you hit this town, it would seem that you have capacity. Your character is something I've got to make snap judgment on. The only concrete thing I've got to go on is collateral. Here is my answer to your loan request. Put up those six double-wagon outfits you say you have coming in, along with those you want to buy, as collateral,

29

and I'll let you have the money.'

It was Cuyler's turn to do a spell of heavy thinking. Those wagons rolling down from Iron Springs represented untold hours of slaving work, of self-denial, of frugal saving to get money enough together to buy them up, one by one. If he agreed to Pomeroy's offer it meant laying on the line everything he possessed in the world. If he lost out in this venture, if he did not win the inevitable fight ahead, then he would be right back where he had started, ten years ago.

Yet, already on this first night in Capell he had, in effect, twice conceivably laid his life on the line. First, when he had moved in, clubbed down Cass Huntoon and faced Huntoon's crowd with a drawn gun. Secondly, when he had ridden down the street, met Ben Loftus and refused to back down. That things had not worked into a shootout in either case could be measured as breaks of the game. Maybe tomorrow, maybe at any time, that shootout would come. It was part of a gamble he had walked into with his eyes open. This whole thing was a gamble and no man ever won a pot by betting on half a card. He faced Pomeroy squarely.

'Fair enough. It's a deal.'

'Good!' said Pomeroy. 'I like your confidence. Drop into the bank at ten o'clock tomorrow morning and the money will be waiting for you.'

In his room, Gene Cuyler had a good wash before turning in for the night. Weary as he was, he lay for some time in thought. It had been a long day and an explosive night. His original intention had been that when he reached Capell he would get the feel of the country and conditions gradually and then lay out his future course of action.

But fate had something to say about that. She had taken him by the crop of the neck and tossed him headfirst into the furiously boiling pot of affairs. In the space of short hours he had made friends and enemies, the latter well outnumbering the former. He had taken a long financial step, laid all that he was and hoped to be on the line. Now, in drowsy reflection he wasn't at all sure whether he'd been a wise man or a fool. It was, he finally concluded, something which only the future could tell.

He got up on one elbow, punched his pillow into a more comfortable shape and went to sleep.

The next morning, down at the corrals, Cuyler found that Mike Kenna had done a good job among the wagon men. Five were willing to sell their outfits and of these, four were open to the proposition of handling a jerkline in Cuyler's employ. The four were Steve Sears, Luke Malcolm, Ott Wylie and Hitch Gower.

Gower was the burly one who had accused Cuyler of being a spy the night before and, while a surly sort, evidently wasn't afraid of a fight, which suited Cuyler all right. He told the five to hook up their outfits and have them on the street in front of the general store by ten o'clock, when he would accept their bills of sale and pay them spot cash. After which they would head out for the ranch country after the first loads of wheat.

The rest of the wagon folk had packed their last belongings and were lining out along the road to Sycamore, beyond the Brushy Hills to the west and south. Watching them go, Cuyler made a silent vow. Before he rode away from these Vaca Plains, whipped as those people were, he'd be buried.

Cuyler went back up town to the big, sprawling general store, against the face of which the new risen sun was pouring its warming rays. Beside the open door a tabby cat dozed and purred contentedly when Cuyler bent to run a caressing hand along the smooth, furred back.

In the doorway stood the proprietor, Gil Saltmarsh, a tall, spare, lantern-jawed man, with keen eyes that reflected a shrewd approach to the world. He spoke drily.

'Glad to see that you're still around this morning, friend. After last night's ruckus and some of the talk I heard around, I expected you'd be hunting more peaceful fields. Think you can stick where the others quit?'

'I expect to,' Cuyler told him. 'I'll have five

wagonloads of wheat rolling for Sycamore today. You got any supplies you want brought back?'

'Plenty!' Gil Saltmarsh snapped the word emphatically. 'I've had a list made up for weeks and getting damn sick and tired of not being able to get the stuff in. I got a business to run here, something which Ben Loftus, Teede Hunnewell and some others can't seem to understand. Virtually all of the staple food used on these plains moves through this store. If those fool cow outfits want to live off a straight beef diet, let 'em. But they've no right to put the pinch on other folks. I got a world of stuff piled up in the River Navigation Company's warehouse at Sycamore. Must be near two full wagonloads of it by this time, and I need all of it—bad! If you keep wagons rolling steady between here and Sycamore, you'll have a regular chunk of good business hauling for me.'

'Give me an authority to pick up your stuff and I'll see that it's brought in for you,' Cuyler promised.

Cuyler was waiting at the door of the bank when it opened at ten o'clock. Pierce Pomeroy, the banker, hailed him with a brisk nod. There were papers all made out and ready for Cuyler's signature. He scanned them briefly, saw that they were in order, and signed.

'As soon as I've paid off for the five outfits I'm buying, I'll bring in the bills of sale and endorse them over to you,' he told Pomeroy.

Pomeroy slid a sack of golden double eagles across the desk. 'Better count it.'

Cuyler did and found it correct. Outside in the street, big Merivale freight wagons were rumbling, heading for the store. Cuyler went to meet them.

On Gil Saltmarsh's counter, Cuyler stacked twenty dollar gold pieces and took in return the bills of sale which were laboriously signed by calloused hands far more agile with a jerkline than with a pen.

Steve Sears gazed at his stack of money admiringly. 'More'n I ever saw in one pile before,' he declared.

Steve was young, clean-cut and curly-headed, with a ready grin and flashing blue eyes. Gil Saltmarsh spoke drily.

'If you're smart, young feller, you'll sock that away and hang on to it. Else the bars and poker tables will eat it up so fast it'll make your head swim.'

Steve grinned. 'That's an idea, Gil. Think I'll let Pierce Pomeroy take care of this for me.'

When Cuyler headed back to the bank, Steve Sears went with him and while the teller took care of Steve, Cuyler endorsed the bills of sale over to Pomeroy as he had promised. Pomeroy stuck out his hand.

'Shake—and good luck!'

Cuyler said, 'This ain't going to make you very popular with the cattle interests,

Pomeroy. It puts you on my side, you know.'

Pomeroy shrugged. 'I'm a banker, first, last and all the time. I'm only concerned in financing what I consider sound business ventures. If a cattleman comes to me for a loan and it is a sound one, I make it. Likewise, if a wheat farmer comes to me for money. So, while I do business with them, why shouldn't I make a loan to you if I see it as a legitimate risk? I run my bank, Cuyler, and let other people run their affairs. Sure, I need the business I get from the cattle interests. But they need me, too, and—' here a faint, enigmatical smile touched his lips—'generally they need me worse than I need them. Don't worry about me. I can take care of myself.'

Steve Sears had finished his business and was carefully tucking away a brand-new deposit book. He grinned at Gene.

'First time I ever tried to save money in my life. Gives me a queer feeling.'

Out in the street a thin, high, mocking yell sounded. Gene and Steve lunged for the door, for that yell was freighted with trouble. And trouble it was.

Down in front of Gil Saltmarsh's store there was battle shaping up. Mike Kenna, Ott Wylie, Hitch Gower and Luke Malcolm stood shoulder to shoulder, facing three times their number of cow hands, who had just ridden into town. The riders had left their horses and were closing in on the wagon men. The leader of

35

them took a swing at Ott Wylie and Ott swung back. The next moment the street was a tangle of savagely fighting men.

With long, loping strides, Gene Cuyler raced toward the melee, Steve Sears pounding staunchly along beside him. The cow hands, Gene saw, were swinging loaded quirt butts as well as their fists. He saw a gun barrel glint in the sun as it rose and fell in a savage, chopping arc. That blow dropped Ott Wylie, cold. And Wylie's outnumbered comrades were being overwhelmed.

Cuyler crashed into the fringe of the fighting tangle, driving for the puncher who had wielded that clubbing gun. He reached a long punch at the fellow, sending him reeling. The next moment a loaded quirt butt thudded against the side of Cuyler's neck, dropping him to his knees, sending a chilling numbness all through him.

It was pretty bad, and grew rapidly worse. For a moment or two after that knockdown, Cuyler was unable to move, though he fought desperately to throw off the paralyzing numbness. He heard a great shout from Steve Sears.

'No you don't, Blaze Doan! Damn you—no you don't!'

He saw Steve dodge that same clubbing quirt butt, saw him dive in and get a grip on his man, wrestle him to the ground and go after him, pounding with both fists. Out of nowhere

36

another cow hand, a late arrival maybe, for he was still in his saddle, drove his horse spinning by. He jerked a foot from the stirrup and drove a wicked kick at Steve Sears. Steve's head snapped sideways and he crumpled in a limp heap.

Sight of that treacherous kick sent a black and blasting rage all through Gene Cuyler, burning away the numbness that had held him powerless. He lurched to his feet, saw a face under a broad hat, hit it. The face disappeared.

The horseman who had kicked Steve, tried to ride Cuyler down. Cuyler barely dodged clear, grabbed at the rider as he flashed by, caught him by the belt and hauled him bodily out of the saddle. He beat a merciless fist into the fellow's face again and again in a cold, concentrated fury.

An avalanche of men hit Cuyler from behind, the sheer weight of them driving him to his knees again. Fists pounded and flailed at him, smashing against his neck, against the back of his head and the numbness began to come back. He managed to turn and the blows took him in the face.

Somehow he got to his feet again, and for a moment beat back his attackers. But only for a moment. There were just too many of them and they came on too savagely. Knotted fists slashed his face, pulped his lips, filled his head with a wild, singing agony. Twice more he went down, twice more he managed somehow to regain his feet.

They had used their boots on him while he was down, kicks drumming against his ribs, his back, his stomach. The kicks in the stomach were the worst, sickening and weakening him. Now, as he stood erect this final time his mouth was open and gasping, and there was the raw, salt harshness of blood in his throat.

His face was streaked with crimson and he fought purely by instinct. But the strength was going out of him and the odds too heavy. He went down again, and the savage, merciless boots went to work on him once more. His senses were slipping, a roaring darkness was reaching for him, sucking him into a mad vortex....

CHAPTER THREE

STERN ISSUE

In a detached, unreal sort of way, Gene Cuyler realized he was struggling desperately to keep that vortex from engulfing him completely. It wasn't a physical fight, it was a mental thing. It was something a man had to set his will against and then hang on. It was a tough fight, but he won it. The vortex gave back and took with it the roaring darkness. The tension ran out of him and he lay there, supine in the dust of the street, sun-scorched dust that clogged his mouth and nose smotheringly. No longer was there the smash of boots against his ribs, nor of fists against his head.

He got spread hands under himself, lifted up to his knees. He stayed there for a time, with a shaky hand mopping the dust and blood out of his eyes. He heard a heavy, splintering crash and some yips of shrill triumph. He was struggling to his feet when a new voice took over in a high, crying indignation and protest.

'Stop it! Don't any of you touch another of those men or their wagons! Uncle Ben, if you don't call them off, I'll never refer to you as my uncle again. I won't live in your house, I won't call you by name. I'll never know you again—if you don't call them off!'

It was the girl of the night before, the girl with the raven black hair. Paula Juilliard. She stood beside a buckboard, her head back, her words lashing at the grizzled, blunt-jawed cattleman who sat on the buckboard seat. Her face was pale, but her dark eyes were blazing.

In his buckboard, Ben Loftus stirred uneasily.

'Now don't you get too worked up, Paula,' he said gruffly. 'Nobody is hurt real bad. And these wagon men, particularly that fellow Cuyler, got to learn—'

'Not hurt real bad!' flared the girl. 'Do you figure no man as really hurt unless he is killed? Look at them!'

She whirled, pointing.

Steve Sears had struggled to a sitting position, his young face pinched and stupefied from that kick in the head. Mike Kenna was on his feet, leaning against a hitch rail, glaring defiance from a bruised and blood-smeared face. Hitch Gower, Ott Wylie and Luke Malcolm were squatted on the edge of the board sidewalk, hunched and sick and beaten. The driver of the fifth wagon, who had agreed to sell, but not to work for Gene Cuyler, stood at the corner of the store. He was a dried-up, leathery little man, by the name of Hack Dowd. There were no marks of combat on him, but there was a strange, set look in his eyes.

These men did Paula Juilliard's pointing finger take in. But mainly that finger seemed to indicate Gene Cuyler who, finally fully on his feet, stood there swaying almost drunkenly, peering around out of battered eyes.

He saw his bloody, beaten men. He saw one wagon, tipped over on its side, with that side splintered and crumpled. Several riders were just loosening their lariats from it. Obviously they had used them, with the pull of their horses at the free ends, to tip the wagon so.

These things Cuyler saw and, deep behind their puffed and swollen lids, his bloodshot eyes went icy. He felt for his gun and found that it was gone. He started for the door of Gil Saltmarsh's store, weaving and stumbling. A cowpuncher lifted a mocking yell.

'There goes your tough guy Mister Cuyler. He's had a big plenty. Yeah, he's had enough!'

Cuyler did not even seem to hear the taunting cry. He kept on moving, his step going a little steadier with each stride. He went into the store, Gil Saltmarsh stepping aside to let him pass.

On one part of the wall behind the store counter was a rack of rifles, with a shelf of ammunition under them. Cuyler reached down a rifle, took a box of ammunition. As he broke open the latter, several long, shining yellow cartridges got away from him and clattered on the floor. He let them go, but hung on to a good handful from the rest of the torn box. He began plugging these through the loading gate of the rifle as he headed for the street again.

Gil Saltmarsh, watching silently up until now, said, 'I don't blame you, Cuyler. But it won't do you any good to get yourself killed. You're one man against better than a dozen.'

Cuyler flashed him a strange, locked look, did not answer. He moved out the door.

A rider was edging in toward another of the freight wagons, swinging the loop of his lariat around his head. The loop snaked out, settled around the jutting top of a side-rack post of the wagon. The rider twitched the loop snug, threw a dally about the horn of his saddle, swung his mount into the beginnings of a pull.

Gene Cuyler's rifle seemed to hardly touch

41

his shoulder before the thin, wicked crash of its report rocketed along the street. The rider's horse collapsed, shot through the head. The rider, startled and cursing, rolled in the dust.

Cuyler never even broke his stride. He racked the lever of the rifle back and forth, jacking a fresh cartridge into the chamber of the weapon. He carried the gun half raised, ready for another instant shot. He threw words ahead of him, in a voice that was hoarse and brittle.

'I'll kill the first man who makes a phony move. Stay put—all of you!'

He moved straight in on the buckboard. Two men sat horses beside the rig. One was a big-nosed, florid-faced man, the other smaller, wiry, swarthy and thin-lipped. The florid-faced man shifted uneasily in his saddle, but the swarthy one faced the threat of Cuyler's rifle with unmoving bleakness. And he spoke, his voice tight and wintry.

'You'll get yourself killed in a minute. All I have to do is give the word. Put that rifle down!'

The muzzle of the rifle looked squarely at the middle of the swarthy one's chest. 'Try speaking that word and you'll be shot in half before you get it past your lips,' Cuyler told him, equally bleak and wintry. Then he drove an order at Ben Loftus.

'You seemed to enjoy seeing that wagon of mine tipped over. Now, them who tipped it over will put it back on its wheels again. Tell 'em to get at it!'

The dark-faced man spoke harshly.

'Don't you soften up now, Loftus, like you did last night. Either for this jingo with his gun, or for that fool niece of yours who don't understand—'

Paula Juilliard had held her place beside the buckboard. Now she whirled on the speaker.

'I understand all I need to, Joe Justin. Which is that neither you or Teede Hunnewell there, or Uncle Ben are lords of the world. I understand that other people have rights and that they deserve fairer treatment than to be mauled and beaten and kicked around because they stand up for those rights. Uncle Ben, tell the hands to put that wagon back on its wheels. Tell them—now!'

Gene Cuyler's twisted grin was more mirthless than a scowl would have been.

'Lady,' he said, 'you've done your best. Now you move on over to the store, so you'll be out of line should these brave buckos need to be convinced—the hard way.' He scrubbed a hand at the blood which slimed his face and the acrid dust which stung his lips and smarted in his eyes.

'No!' She swung out to face him and she caught her breath as she marked the deep lines carved about his mouth, put there in such brief time by the accumulated torture of flesh and spirit from the beating he'd taken. She stammered slightly. 'Your wagon—I'll see that it's righted—and I'll pay for the damage done it. Only, let this thing stop here, once and for all.'

Cuyler shook his head. 'Money might pay for a smashed wagon, but never for the rest of this. When a man is beaten like a dog, then he pays back in kind. These brave saddle pounders are going to pay, my way. Please—get out of line!'

From the moment they recovered from the first cold shock when Gene Cuyler's flashing shot had dropped the horse of one of their number, the riders had been spreading out and around, taut and ready. Ben Loftus saw this and he saw that Gene Cuyler would never back down. A word, a sudden motion and this thing could be a very deadly explosion. Which was bad enough, even if Paula Juilliard were not right in the middle of things. But she was, and she wouldn't leave. To ward this thing off, somebody had to give in. Ben Loftus did.

He waved an arm. 'Break it up!' he called to the riders. 'Forget your guns. Put that wagon back on its wheels!'

Joe Justin, swarthy and suddenly malevolent, twisted in his saddle, swinging his horse around so suddenly it jammed a shoulder into Paula Juilliard, sending her staggering. Justin had dropped a hand to the gun he wore and his voice lashed at Ben Loftus.

'You soft fool! I always knew that you'd turn

44

spineless in a pinch. Maybe you're backing down, but I'm not!'

He whirled his horse back, opened his mouth to yell at the riders. That was when Gene Cuyler moved in, the barrel of his rifle swinging. It caught Joe Justin across the side of the head and brought him soddenly out of his saddle.

Behind Cuyler sounded Steve Sears' voice, a little thick but taut with resolve.

'Stay with 'em, Gene! I found your gun and I'm backing your hand. Stay with 'em!'

It was florid-faced Teede Hunnewell who swung the thin balance. It wasn't necessarily any sense of fairness or justice that decided Hunnewell. The thing that really moved Hunnewell was that there was Joe Justin, senseless on the ground and now this beaten, bloody-faced fellow with the rifle, Gene Cuyler, was looking at him. And behind Cuyler was Steve Sears moving up, a dusty six-shooter in his fist. If things broke wide open, then one thing was almost sure, regardless of the over-all outcome of affairs. He, Teede Hunnewell, would almost certainly stop a slug. So now he raised a yell.

'Loftus is right! Straighten that wagon up and let's get out of here!'

Gene Cuyler and Steve Sears stood shoulder to shoulder, a little oasis of deathless defiance in the middle of this dusty street. They watched the sullen, reluctant cow hands gather about the tipped-over wagon and begin to right it. It took the combined efforts of straining men, lunging horses and singing tight lariats to do the job.

When this was done, Teede Hunnewell called a rider over to help him get Joe Justin into his saddle, where he swayed drunkenly, only half conscious. Hunnewell mounted, prepared to ride slowly out of town, holding Joe Justin from toppling again into the dust. Gene Cuyler made a short, abrupt move with his rifle.

'You're not done yet, Hunnewell. You can't leave that dead horse in the middle of the street. Do something about it!'

Teede Hunnewell gritted his teeth and his florid face flamed even more redly. This, Cuyler knew, was pouring it on, but it was his mood at the moment and he was implacable. Hunnewell snapped an order to the riders and they gathered around the dead animal, stripping off saddle and other gear. Then two of them set loops about the hind legs of the horse, set their ponies to the pull and moved slowly off along the street, the drag of the carcass building up a haze of dust.

'Anything else?' snarled Hunnewell.

Cuyler's hard grin was a grimace. 'You can go now.'

They went, all of those in saddle. Left now of the cattle crowd was only Ben Loftus in his buckboard and the tall, black-haired girl who

46

had taken her place beside him. Cuyler stepped closer to the buckboard.

'A moment, Loftus—and a final word.'

Cuyler dropped his rifle across his arm, so that it was no longer a threat. He looked Loftus squarely in the eye.

'You and your crowd started this, Loftus. All in all, my side got the worst of the round. If I'm any judge of pig-headed, obstinate men, there'll be other rounds coming up. If and when they do, it won't be me and my men who start the trouble. But we've taken all of this sort of trouble we're going to. Next time, there will be just one answer. This!' He patted the breech of his rifle. 'I'm hanging one of these on every one of my wagons. Me and my men are never going to take another physical beating. If your crowd ever again try to hand us one, there'll be dead men on the ground. Think on that—think on it, hard!'

'If you had any sense,' rapped Loftus, 'you'd never have moved into our affairs here on the Vaca Plains, Cuyler. Why don't you hunt some other place to set up your freight route? You'll never make a go of it here.'

'Never is a long time,' Cuyler retorted. 'And it is a free country. I'm going to stick, Loftus. Frankly, I'd a lot rather be friends with you people than an enemy. I hope to see the day come when that will be possible. I'd like to start now—with you.'

Loftus stirred, cleared his throat harshly.

47

'Not a chance. You're in the wrong game to be a friend of mine. Last night and today should have made that plain. This much I will say. I hate to see a man with your measure of nerve taken apart. Yet that will come unless you listen to reason and get off these plains with your wagons.'

Cuyler looked at Paula Juilliard. This black-haired girl had a quick, vivid beauty, with a high measure of balance and reserve behind it. She held the directness of Cuyler's glance for a moment, then colored and looked away.

'Last night,' observed Cuyler quietly, 'I heard Jim Nickerson say that Miss Juilliard had more sense in her pretty head than any of you men in the cow business have shown so far. From what I saw and heard then, and here today, I agree with him. I hope she manages to pass on some of her savvy to the rest of you.'

A deepening wave of color ran up the girl's slender, sunbrowned throat. She spoke stiffly.

'I'm for cattle and the rights of cattlemen, all the way.'

'Fine!' nodded Cuyler. 'So am I. But I'm for the rights of other men, too—including my own.'

Ben Loftus spun the buckboard and drove off along the street, pulling in in front of Pierce Pomeroy's bank. Watching, Cuyler saw both Loftus and the girl get down and go in. Just before she entered, Paula Juilliard turned her head and looked back. Cuyler lifted a hand in ironic salute. The sunlight glinted on the girl's black head as she jerked swiftly around and went on into the bank.

Cuyler turned back to his own crowd. He looked at Steve Sears beside him and said, 'How are you, kid?'

Steve's face had a drained, sick look, but he managed a ghost of his old, cheery smile. 'Still pretty much in one piece and still with you, Gene.'

Mike Kenna's growl came rumbling. 'And here, lad!'

There was no such encouraging response from the other three, who had the old, dejected, whipped look about them. Ott Wylie was mumbling, 'Life's too short to go on taking this sort of thing—'

Cuyler saw Luke Malcolm nod dazed agreement to this. Hitch Gower just hunched sullenly, dabbing at his battered mouth.

Cuyler went into the store and faced Gil Saltmarsh. 'Guns,' he said. 'Rifles just like this one. Half a dozen of them, with ammunition.'

The storekeeper nodded and began lifting the weapons out of the rack, laying them on the counter and stacking boxes of ammunition beside them. From a corner he brought leather scabbards.

'Without a scabbard a gun goes to hell fast, kicking about a wagon. These are on the house.'

'This is none of your pie,' reminded Cuyler.

'No?' Gil Saltmarsh swore, low and angry. 'The dammed, arrogant fools! Who do they think they are, pushing the rights of other people around this way? You bet this is some of my pie!'

'Not a lick of sense in you getting them on your neck, too,' Cuyler cautioned.

Saltmarsh slammed a vehement fist on the counter. 'I don't owe any of them one thin dime. This store feeds and supplies a lot of people besides cow outfits, and it's my living. If freight wagons don't roll, then I can't do business, people don't eat and I go busted. Those three, Loftus and Hunnewell and Justin, can bring in their own supplies by pack train or in a wagon of their own, maybe. But how about me, and other folks?'

'I'll bring your supplies in,' said Cuyler grimly.

'Exactly! So, for what I'm worth, Cuyler, I'm backing you. You took a licking out there, but I can see you're not through. You got guts and I'm for you, in any way I can help. To hell with Loftus and Hunnewell and Justin! I tell you, these scabbards are on the house!'

With Saltmarsh helping, Cuyler carried the rifles outside. He handed one to Mike Kenna, another to Steve Sears and offered one to Ott Wylie, saying, 'We never take another manhandling from that gang, boys.'

Ott Wylie refused the rifle, shaking his head. 'Not for me. I'm whipped all to hell, know it

50

and admit it. I'm through!'

'You can give me that gun, Cuyler,' said a voice from behind.

It was leathery little Hack Dowd. 'When you paid me off for my outfit,' he went on, 'I headed right down to the hotel to buy a stage ticket for Sycamore. I figured I was all through in these parts. I was at the hotel when the ruckus started. Time I got back it was just about all over. I've changed my mind, Cuyler. I want to run a jerkline for you and have a share in licking those damn bullying cattlemen.'

Gene Cuyler handed over the gun. 'I don't mind taking a licking, Hack, if it puts a man like you on my side.'

Ott Wylie blurted a harsh, 'Ah—what the hell! If Hack Dowd can feel that way, I reckon I can. Gimme a gun!'

Luke Malcolm spat painfully, managed a crooked grin. 'It's a devil of a way to earn a living, but if Ott can stand it, I ought to be able to. I'm game to try 'em another round.'

Which left only Hitch Gower, who was staring at the empty street with blank, deadly eyes.

'I'll take a gun,' he said thickly. 'I'll load it up and the first damn cow hand who looks slantwise at me, I'll blow his head off.'

'I'm giving you a rifle,' said Cuyler. 'But use your head with it. These guns are just to make sure they don't tackle us this way again.'

51

* * *

Survey of the wagon that had been overturned showed side racks smashed, the reach splintered and an axle twisted out of line. Considerable repair was necessary before this wagon would roll again, earning its keep. It was a pretty heavy body blow at this time, when Cuyler needed every cent of revenue he could scrape up.

They got the wagon down to the corrals. Steve Sears, though gamely doing his part, was still plainly suffering a lot from that kick in the head. So Cuyler ordered him to lie around, take it easy and just keep an eye on things in general. Luke Malcolm, a good hand with the tools, offered to start repair work on the damaged wagon and Gene told him to go to it. Then, saddling up his horse, Gene headed out for the wheat ranches, followed by the other four wagons, with Mike Kenna, Ott Wylie, Hack Dowd and Hitch Gower at the jerklines.

The road led across the flat plains to a country of huge, fenced fields, where wheat was growing toward rich and ripe maturity, vast acres of it, rippling like a green and shining sea before the push of a slow, warm breeze. The breath of those fat fields was heavy in the air, brave with promise.

There was a big, solid gate at the entrance to the Nickerson farm. And there was a man guarding it, a rifle across his arm.

'Something you wanted?' he challenged.

'Yeah,' Gene Cuyler told him. 'We've come to haul wheat. I told Nickerson I'd be out.'

The guard stripped a heavy lock and chain from the gate.

'Four wagons won't begin to handle Nickerson's wheat, let alone that of Abe Pettibone, Mark Travis and some of the rest.'

'There'll be more wagons,' Cuyler promised.

They rolled down the side road, with the verdant wheat fields pushing in on either hand. Cuyler thought of that armed guard and a chained gate, fitting symbol of conditions across these wide plains. Every move a man made, it seemed, meant battle or obstruction.

Half a mile along, farm buildings loomed. Cuyler, spurring out ahead, saw the big, burly figure of Jim Nickerson coming to meet him, a wide grin on his face.

'I was hoping, Cuyler,' he rumbled, 'but holding my thumbs. This way if you want to see wheat.' His glance fixed on Cuyler's battered face. 'Sa-ay, you look like there might have been a little trouble along the way.'

Cuyler nodded. 'A little.' He outlined briefly the highlights of the fight in town. 'Next time,' he ended, 'things will be different. There's a rifle riding on every wagon from now on, and not as an ornament.'

'Seems the cattle crowd won't be satisfied until they bring things to a shootout,' said Nickerson soberly. 'And the thought scares me. I've always lived in hopes that someway, somehow, we'd be able to square things all around by peaceful means. I dunno.' He shook his head.

Cuyler built a cigarette, peeled his bruised lips back slightly as the first smoke stung them. 'I had a chance to look the big three over today, Loftus, Hunnewell and Justin. I had the feeling that given time a man might make peace with Ben Loftus. But Teede Hunnewell, I wouldn't trust him three jumps. And Justin is bad—dangerous. How close am I shootin'?'

'About right,' agreed Nickerson. 'Loftus has been in my hair several times, but I've always felt that it was more because Justin and Hunnewell were pushing him at me than because he liked to raise hell. I'd say that, over all, Loftus is a square shooter. Teede Hunnewell is a slick, ruthless schemer. And Justin is just what you said he was, dangerous.'

There was a big, gaunt, red-painted barn, piled to the rafters with sacked wheat. Tons on tons of it. Gene Cuyler was impressed.

'Wheat to move, all right. In the face of the cattle crowd's opposition, how'd you ever manage to haul in enough lumber to build a layout like this?'

Nickerson shrugged. 'They didn't bother us at first. Figured this country was a little too dry to grow good wheat crops. So if we wanted to go about building up a lot of ranches we'd go broke on, that was our hard luck and poor judgement. But there was a lot they didn't know about wheat, like that dry country, drought-resistant strain of wheat that had been developed back in Kansas. We brought in some of that particular seed and by the time the opposition woke up to what was going on, we were dug in too deep to be rooted out without a bigger battle than they've so far wanted to try. But things are building up. It's got to come to a final showdown, one way or the other. I hate to see that day arrive, but when it does I'll be in there, doing my best.'

Nickerson called up several ranch hands and, one after another, the four wagons were loaded with sacked wheat. There was a cut-off through a back field which would enable the wagons to hit the Sycamore road without going back through town.

With Mike Kenna in charge and at the jerkline of the lead wagon, the four big Merivales lined out, heavy and slow, the yoke bells of the leaders of each mule team jangling and clashing musically. They looked good to Gene Cuyler. Here was the real start of his big venture. Wagons on the road, loaded and rolling.

He thought of other wagons coming in, down along the Fort Rutledge road. Tonight they should be in Capell, some time tonight; and it would be a good idea to get back to town and see that things were in readiness for their arrival.

Nickerson walked over to his horse with him. 'This is a sort of mutual proposition,' said the wheat-rancher. 'I need you and you need me. You can count on my all-out backing, Cuyler. I know I speak for Abe Pettibone and Mark Travis, too. You stick by us, we'll stick by you, through thick and thin. It's the only way we can hope to whip our common trouble. Watch yourself. You made Hunnewell and Justin crawl today. They'll never forget or never forgive. Good luck!'

CHAPTER FOUR

DEATH IN THE NIGHT

The freight corrals at the south end of Capell which the wagon men had been using, were sprawling and roomy. There were several big oaks in them which threw spreading shade and under these were a couple of long watering troughs, fed by pipes from a lazily spinning windmill, which squealed forlornly on each upstroke. About the dark wetness of the overflow from the troughs, blackbirds perched and fluttered, their chirping clear and bell-like.

West of the corrals ran a long, low building of adobe, built by that Spanish don of long ago. It was considerably the worse from neglect and the remorseless toll of the years, yet

Gene Cuyler saw that with some lumber and work it could be made into a very acceptable office and storehouse and bunkhouse for his men. The corrals were in pretty good shape, as were the feed sheds, having been at least sketchily repaired and maintained by other wagon men from time to time.

Cuyler had no idea who, if anyone, held title to the property on which the corrals stood. Maybe Pierce Pomeroy would be able to tell him, which was something it would be wise to find out about before spending too much money on repairs. From past experience Gene knew that many freight corrals and wagon camps were public property, free to the use of any wagon man. Isolated towns and communities, dependent on those rolling, dusty wagons for supplies and freight, were in most cases only too glad to supply accommodations for the freighters. This might be different. It was something to check up on.

Luke Malcolm was already at work on the damaged wagon, blocking it up so that the broken reach might be replaced and the sprung axle taken off and straightened. Steve Sears was helping him, but Steve did not look so good. His eyes were bloodshot and his face overly flushed.

'I told you to take it easy, kid,' said Cuyler gruffly. 'A kick in the head like you took could turn out bad. You go up to my room at the hotel and turn in. What you need is a good sleep. Go get it, and no argument!'

Steve rubbed a hand across his eyes. 'I'm all right, except I go a little dizzy now and then.'

'Which is just why you need rest. Scatter along!'

Cuyler unsaddled and turned his horse into the corrals and then, increasingly aware of the dismal squeal of the windmill, located a half-filled can of axle grease in a rack on the side of the damaged wagon, climbed the ladder of the windmill tower and began daubing grease on dry cogs and pump-rod slides.

Busy at this, with the whir and clank of the mill in his ears, he did not notice the approaching rider until she pulled to a halt right below him. He looked down at a bared yellow head, a smooth brown forehead and the tip of a sun-browned nose. She was swinging her head from side to side, almost warily, as her glance ran here and there.

Cuyler smiled slightly and called down, 'Hi!'

The yellow head tilted back and startled blue eyes looked up at him.

'Looking for somebody?' Cuyler asked. 'Maybe me?'

He saw her slim, child-like throat work as she gulped down her surprise.

'Wh-what are you doing up there?' she stammered.

'Spreading a little well-needed grease. This mill had a squeal to it like a hog under a gate.'

Cuyler swung down the ladder and stood

58

facing her. She had recovered her composure and was staring at him with open hostility, though a shaded uncertainty still lurked in her blue eyes.

'You, of course,' drawled Cuyler, 'are Candy Loftus.'

The yellow head gave a slight nod.

'And you,' she retorted, 'are this impossible Gene Cuyler person.'

'Right! Which practically introduces us,' Cuyler grinned.

'You don't,' said Candy Loftus bluntly, 'look like such a much.'

'I'm not,' agreed Cuyler. 'Just an ordinary sort of a cluck, trying to get along. What did you expect, anyhow—somebody nine feet high and five feet across the shoulders?'

'I wasn't exactly sure,' she told him stiffly. 'But I wanted a good look, in broad daylight, at the person who clubbed Cass Huntoon out of his saddle, made Blaze Doan back down, made pretty much of a fool out of Dad in front of the hotel last night, and ended up by taking a good licking in front of Gil Saltmarsh's store this morning, even though you did follow that up by bluffing everybody out with a rifle. Finally,' she ended scathingly, 'for some silly reason I can't understand, you seem to have that fool cousin of mine, Paula Juilliard, all in a dither. No, I can't understand that, for now that I've had a good look at you, you're not such a much. Just an ordinary pig-headed,

59

mule-chasing wagon man.'

She amused Cuyler, for there was so much of a wilful, headstrong, spoiled child about her. Even so, the scorn behind her words carried a bite.

'Let's make this even,' Cuyler drawled. 'You've read my pedigree, now I'll read yours. I'd say that you were just an ornery little brat, selfish as sin, spoiled all to thunder, badly in need of having half a dozen switches worn out on you. A chore which your pa has too long neglected and which I should have taken care of for him with that quirt, last night. You sure had it coming to you, Candy Loftus.'

'Which is nothing to what you have coming to you,' she blazed back. 'And what you'll get, Mister Gene Cuyler. If you had any sense you'd have learned from that walloping you got this morning, cleared out of this country and stayed out. But you didn't—so you'll see!'

'For a taffy-headed kid,' mocked Cuyler teasingly, 'you're the most bloodthirsty little savage I ever ran up against. Did Papa tell you to come and give me this warning?'

'He did not!'

Cuyler saw the anger sizzle in her eyes, watched her face pale with it. He laughed.

'Candy Loftus. Pretty as a thistle patch in bloom. But just as stickery and just as useless.'

For a moment he thought she was going to ride him down, so furious was she. But abruptly she spun her pony and raced away, yellow hair streaming like a banner behind her.

Flat on his back, over under the damaged wagon, Luke Malcolm laughed softly. 'I'd say you kinda won that round, Gene. But she'll sure have it in for you now. Sure is a fiery little scalawag and doesn't rate us wagon men more'n half a jump above a rattlesnake in a wagon track.'

'Seems to be a pretty common opinion in the cattle circles,' admitted Cuyler drily. 'Let's hope the time'll come when it'll be different. Here, I'll give you a hand with that reach.'

Cuyler stayed, helping Luke with the wagon until the afternoon had pretty much run away. Then he went up town and looked in at his room to see how Steve Sears was doing. Steve was sound asleep. The feverish flush had left his face and the drawn lines of shock and pain about his mouth had relaxed. Steve would wake up his old, buoyant self.

Feeling much better about the kid, Cuyler washed away all removable signs of conflict from his own bruised and swollen face, ate supper, found a round-backed chair on one end of the hotel porch and slouched there at ease, smoking.

A soft, blue twilight lay over this town of Capell, steadily deepening. Cuyler watched the town come to life in the welcome coolness of dusk and presently identified Pierce Pomeroy as the latter came down the street from the bank where he'd apparently been working late.

61

As Pomeroy climbed the hotel steps, Cuyler called to him and the banker came over. Cuyler explained about the freight corral layout.

'To handle the number of wagon outfits I expect to build up, considerable fixing around the corrals will have to be done. The corrals proper will have to be enlarged and that old adobe building cleaned up and repaired for quarters for my men. There'll be more feed sheds needed. I don't want to sink too much money into such things unless I can depend on using the layout permanently. Most places I've worked out of, the corrals and wagon park were pretty much public property, free to the use of any and everyone. But I want to be sure about this one.'

Pomeroy listened quietly, shook his head.

'Off hand I can't say just who does hold title to that property, if anyone does. I'll see if I can find out. If there is any owner, I doubt you'll have any trouble working out a satisfactory deal. I'd say you'll be perfectly safe in going ahead with any improvements you figure necessary. How badly did that cattle crowd damage that wagon they turned over?'

'Not too bad. It'll be rolling again in a couple of days. Biggest loss is the revenue it could have earned had it been carrying a load of wheat out to Sycamore along with the other four.'

'I was wondering if the other four were on their way,' said Pomeroy. 'Who's in charge?'

'Mike Kenna.'

Pomeroy nodded. 'A good man. That was quite a ruckus you fellows went through this morning, wasn't it?' He dropped a hand on Cuyler's shoulder. 'I liked the way you made Hunnewell and Loftus and Joe Justin crawl. I'm feeling better about this thing all the time.'

Cuyler rubbed a hand gently over his battered face. 'I don't mind taking a licking once in a while. But that deal this morning was pretty rugged, for a fact. It would have been a lot worse if that girl, Paula Juilliard hadn't stepped in. She sure saved our skins.'

Pierce Pomeroy stirred slightly. 'Four wagonloads of wheat over the road are better than nothing.'

'That's right. By this time next week it'll be four times four. Even if we have to shoot our way down every mile of road.'

Pomeroy nodded. 'That's the stuff.' He went on into the hotel.

The night deepened. A little breeze crept around the corner of the hotel, dry and sweet from its run across miles of plains land still warm from the late departed sun. Over at the edge of town some kids were at play, their carefree shouts and laughter lifting clear. A dog, playing with them, barked excitedly. Against the contrast of the velvet dark, windows and open doorways were squares and rectangles of golden light.

Gene Cuyler thought again of those wagons

63

of his that were rolling down from Iron Springs. Some time tonight or early tomorrow morning they should be in. He was impatient for their arrival, for they were the truly solid background of this whole venture. Their arrival would mean that wheat would start rolling down the miles to Sycamore as it had never rolled before. Their arrival meant six more men to back his hand, tough fighting men, tried and true. With these wagons and these men on hand there would be a bulk and solidity to his enterprise that might very well make the cattle crowd stop, look and listen a long time before starting any more trouble. Yeah, it sure would be good when his old tried outfit of wagons and men got in.

Cuyler tipped his head and listened to a sound which carried in across the night. Not yet in town, but closing fast. The drumbeat of racing hoofs. Cuyler straightened a little in his chair. One horse, it sounded like, running all out. It could mean something, or nothing. Candy Loftus, it seemed, always rode that way, helter-skelter, tawny hair flying. . . .

The horse raced into the upper end of the street, fled down along it and slid to a halt in front of the hotel. Spurs jingled as the rider swung from the saddle and ran up the steps. The light flare from the door brought that rider into sharp relief, and Gene Cuyler got to his feet. The rider was Paula Juilliard!

Her black hair had pulled loose and lay over

64

her shoulders, fluffed and tangled from the wind of hard riding. She ran swiftly into the hotel and Cuyler could hear a sharp note of urgency in her voice as she called to Sam Reeves, the hotelkeeper.

There was the murmur of voices, blunted and made unintelligible by the barrier of walls. Then the girl was out on the porch again, swinging her head from side to side as she searched the darkness of the street in obvious desperation.

'Gene Cuyler—I've got to find him!' she was crying softly to herself. 'I've got to—for they're close behind—!'

Cuyler called quietly. 'Over here, Miss Juilliard. You want—me?'

She came so fast she nearly ran into him and Cuyler dropped a hand on her shoulder to steady her.

'Quick!' she panted. 'You've got to go—get out of town!'

'Steady!' murmured Cuyler. 'What's wrong?'

'Teede Hunnewell, Joe Justin—maybe Uncle Ben—and a good dozen more. They're coming to get you. You hear me—coming with guns and they mean to shoot you on sight. I heard them planning this. This time it won't be just a manhandling. This time they intend to finish you, and you'll have no chance against so many of them. Please—you must hurry, for they have Gatt Ivance with them!'

65

A ripple of tensing movement went all through Cuyler.

'Gatt Ivance! There's only one Gatt Ivance. The gun-fighter. I thought I'd seen the last of him in that Burney trouble. Now he's here—on these Vaca Plains?'

'Of course!' cried the girl. 'He's a new hand of Joe Justin's and they mean to throw him at you. He's deadly. Won't you hurry? You've got to ride for it—now!'

Cuyler growled a thought aloud. 'No, I'll not run from Gatt Ivance. The last time it was Ivance who ran from me.'

Paula Juilliard was almost whimpering as she beat slim, clenched fists against his chest.

'Don't be an idiot! No matter what you did in the past, this time you'll have no chance. They intend to hunt you down like a cornered animal. More than a dozen of them, besides Ivance. Oh, please! Get on your horse and ride, at least for tonight. Somewhere—anywhere out of town where they can't find you. How can I—make—him—understand—?'

Her words ran off in a little wail of desperation. A vague and elusive fragrance lifted from the disorder of her wind-blown hair and it lifted the beat of Gene Cuyler's pulse.

'Just why did you come to warn me?' he asked. 'You owe me nothing. So—why?'

'Does that matter?' she cried. 'I don't know why I came. I just had to, for some reason. To stop what would be—murder. And now you

66

won't listen to me. I've done no good it seems, unless you'll go— Ah—too late—too late—!'

Cuyler heard them at the same moment. Hoofs racing into town—from both ends of the street. Slowing the moment they reached the outskirts, then coming on at a more measured pace that was even more ominous than haste. From both ends of town they were closing in, and he was between them. Even had he wanted to, he couldn't get to his horse, for some of those shadowy riders were between him and the freight corrals. They had him trapped.

Paula Juilliard began to sob, very softly.

This south end of the hotel porch, where Gene Cuyler had been sitting, was darker than the north end. Close to the hotel wall the gloom lay thick, for the porch-overhang blotted out the light of the new stars. Cuyler moved softly into that deeper gloom, drawing the girl with him.

He could feel her trembling, there in the circle of his arm, her slimness taut with desperation.

'No tears,' he murmured. 'This hand hasn't been fully dealt yet. They're a long way from getting me.'

'But they will. They'll search every corner, every shadow of this town. They're up on their fastest horses, to ride you down if they have to. Won't you go?—quickly!'

'Couldn't get to my horse, now. It's in the freight corrals and they've got me blocked off

67

from there. We'll wait this out a little longer.'

'Take my horse. It's very fast.'

'And have them turn on you? No.'

'They'd do nothing to me. They wouldn't dare. You know that. So take my horse and ride for it.'

'Maybe later. Not now, for the setup isn't right. I've got to wait for the break, for the chance. This is the third time you've moved to help me, Paula Juilliard. Why?' His arm tightened about her.

'Hush!' she warned softly. But she made no move to draw away.

The clump of hoofs was close now. Cuyler could see them in the pale starlight, two dark blots of riders, moving in from either end of the street. A growling voice ran across the night, Joe Justin's voice.

'Far enough! Stay put until I see if he's in the hotel. I understand Sam Reeves rented him a room. Ivance, you come with me.'

The two of them dismounted, close to Paula Juilliard's horse. A hard, toneless voice said, 'Whose bronc is that?'

'Not Cuyler's. His is down in the freight corrals. Come on!'

They clanked up the steps and across the porch to the door, full in the light flare. Joe Justin led, swarthy and thin-lipped, the glint of a bandage showing under his hat. The man with him made a gaunt, high-shouldered figure.

His lips almost touching her ear, Gene Cuyler breathed, 'The same Gatt Ivance. He's bad, but I made him cut and run, out of the Burney lumber fight.'

She lifted a soft palm, pressed it against his lips, silencing him.

Joe Justin's voice made a hard droning as he called for Sam Reeves. Cuyler heard the hotelkeeper answer and there was an exchange of angry words. There was no clear content to them but soon Justin and Ivance stamped back across the porch and down the steps to the street, when Justin began giving harsh orders.

'He's about town somewhere. Comb the whole layout. Don't overlook the store. Saltmarsh favors him, which is something I'll take up with Saltmarsh later. Doan, you and Huntoon get back to the freight corrals and see that he doesn't sneak his horse out. Rest of you comb this town. Smoke him down on sight. He's dangerous!'

Cuyler brushed his lips free of Paula Juilliard's silencing palm, buried them for a moment in the fragrant glory of her wind tossed hair. Then he murmured, 'This is the break. Don't move a step, not even a finger. And bless you—!'

He moved away from her, a drifting shadow. Out there in the street men were dismounting, spurs clanking and jangling. For this moment, sound and movement were everywhere and Cuyler was making the most of it. He threaded the blackness along the hotel wall to the very end of the porch and let himself softly off the end of it. There, low-crouched, he waited.

His pulse was hammering. Not altogether because of the bleak danger which lay on every side of him, but because of that strange and gallant girl back there. The fragrance of her hair was still in his nostrils—

On one point he knew tremendous relief. Now, if gunplay started, he was far enough away from Paula Juilliard to leave her in little danger of some wild-flying slug. Paula, this strange and lovely girl of the cattle land, who had ridden to warn him, who had been so close to him, right in the circle of his arm, her soft palm against his lips. . . .

He shook his head, almost angrily. He had to bring his thoughts back to the danger which stalked the night after him, deadly and purposeful.

Crouched there at the end of the porch, he tried to figure this thing out. They had come to ride him down, if they had to. They were up on their fastest horses. So Paula Juilliard had told him. Corner him and smoke him down in town if they could, ride him down if he managed to slip away and make a run for it. Even if he did get clear of town, that would not mean escape. They'd be after him.

Still, that was the only chance. To try and remain in town was to be surely found, sooner or later. They'd stay on after him all night, if

70

they had to, and renew their search in the morning light. So he had to get out of town, and there was that horse of Paula Juilliard's, if he could get it unobserved and then manage some sort of break. But if he rode, what direction would he take?

Just a wild, aimless dash wouldn't do. Too much hung in the balance. This was life—or death. He had to think this thing out clearly.

And then he remembered!

Somewhere out on the old Fort Rutledge road, wagons were rolling. His wagons, his men, coming down across the Vaca Plains to this town of Capell. They might be just a few miles out, they might be many. But once he reached them, then Justin and Hunnewell and Loftus and all these others could have all the fight they wanted. That, he decided, was his only chance; it was what he had to do, ride to meet the wagons. But first he had to get out of town, with a fast-running horse under him!

He waited, watching and listening, every sense leaping and alive. He saw men spreading up and down the street, all but two of them on foot now. The mounted two rode south along the street. Blaze Doan and Cass Huntoon, riding to guard against any chance of his getting to his horse in the freight corrals.

It was as tight a corner, Cuyler knew, as he had ever been up against in all his life. He heard the bleak growl of Joe Justin's voice, giving more orders. Justin was almost directly across

71

the street from him. Cuyler edged further out from the corner of the hotel porch, searching the street with straining eyes and ears. He located men by the jangle of their spurs, by the guarded rumble of their voices. They were scattering everywhere, it seemed—these men who were setting out with such cold-blooded purpose to kill him. But in this gloom, how could they quickly and surely identify him from one of their own crowd?

It would be gambling, but gambling boldly. He didn't need much time, just a few short seconds. He was going to gamble that recognition would not come until those seconds were used up. He drew his gun, straightened and walked with slow deliberation toward Paula Juilliard's horse. This was it!

He reached the girl's horse, caught up the down-dropped reins. That was when, close beside him, a hard, toneless voice lashed at him.

'You! Who are you—?'

Cuyler was turning at the first word. Where this man had come from so suddenly, he did not know. But there the man was, a gaunt, high-shouldered figure; menacing under the stars.

Gatt Ivance!

'Why,' murmured Cuyler, in a disarming drawl, 'I'm just—Cuyler!'

Even as he spoke, Cuyler was leaping in, his

gun swung high. He could have easily beaten the gunman to the shot this time. But a shot would bring them swarming, for it would be a crashing alarm. And Cuyler needed precious seconds to be up and riding before the alarm broke. So he wanted to keep this as silent as he could.

He knew that Ivance was whipping out a gun, knew that this gaunt gunman was very, very fast. It all hung in a thread-thin measure of time. Cuyler's gun was lashing down, the blow aimed at Ivance's head. It thudded solidly home and the gunman crumpled, but with a trained reflex that would not be denied, Gatt Ivance, even as he fell, drove a crashing shot into the street in front of him.

Paula Juilliard's horse, already startled and edgy, moved to whirl away. Cuyler grabbed for the saddle horn, barely caught it and hung on as the lunging horse dragged him several yards before Cuyler could, by desperate effort, get his feet under him and make a wild leap for the saddle. He got a leg over, rode out a few more jumps that way before he could get fully astride. Then he lay far out over the horse's neck, grabbing for the dangling, whipping reins.

Luckily the animal was headed north along the street and it was luck for Cuyler that in his effort to catch the reins, he was flattened along the animal's neck, for already the shooting had started and lead was whimpering by overhead.

Cuyler got the reins, had the horse under control at last, and now rode for it.

Behind him he heard the thin wild anger of Joe Justin raging along the street, ahead an answering shout by Teede Hunnewell, and everywhere gunfire. Cuyler clung to one hope—that this horse would not be hit. And it wasn't—but he was!

It was as though someone had struck at him with a white-hot iron, high up along the heavy muscles of his left arm, a jerk that left a streak of searing fire there.

Ahead, from either side of the street, men were running out to try and block his flight, their guns spitting pale flame. Cuyler shot back, saw a running figure stumble and fall. Gun flame stabbed straight ahead and a wisp of the horse's tossing mane whipped back into Cuyler's face, cut off by a bullet as cleanly as scissors might have done it. Cuyler rode down the man behind that gun, saw the fellow try to dodge clear. But the horse's off shoulder caught him and knocked him end over end into the dust.

Now, abruptly, all the yelling and shooting were behind Cuyler, and the last of the town buildings flashed by. Ahead was the open starlit night, the wide, beckoning plains. He'd done it! The desperate break he'd planned had carried him through. If they wanted him now they'd have to outride him, run him down. His exultation was too great to hold in. He turned

74

his head and sent echoing back a long, taunting yell of triumph and defiance.

The sound of that yell affected many people in many different ways. Joe Justin was raging and cursing as he called on his men for pursuit. Teede Hunnewell, lying on the street with a leg shattered by a slug from Gene Cuyler's gun, echoed Justin's curses, with an added note of helplessness.

Over at the hotel, Paula Juilliard moved to the outer edge of the porch, her eyes wide and shining and speaking her thoughts aloud.

'Let Goldie run, Gene—let him run! They'll never catch you if you'll just let him run!'

Inside a darkened and partly opened window of the hotel, right in back of Paula, Pierce Pomeroy stood, silent. He had been there all the time, when the girl had first brought her warning to Gene Cuyler and when, in the circle of Cuyler's arm, she had crouched there in the gloom with him, measuring his chances, waiting for the break. Pomeroy had heard the words that passed between them and he heard the girl's unconsciously spoken thoughts now, gauging the emotion and relief behind them which told far more than the words themselves.

Pomeroy's face was locked, the corners of his mouth white with repression, his black eyes blank. He had an unlighted perfecto in his lips, an unlighted match in his hand. The muscles along his jaw bunched suddenly and the

75

perfecto, bitten cleanly through, fell to the floor. His white fingers writhed and the match broke with a tiny snap. He turned away from the window, silent as a shadow.

*   *   *

Out in the rushing night, Gene Cuyler had straightened in the saddle, gauging the stride of the horse under him. It was swift, smooth and powerful, with no faltering or break in it anywhere, which would have been evident had the animal been hit. There were, Cuyler knew, horses that were very fast for a short distance, but which lacked bottom, staying power. Then there were others which had not only speed, but ran with a rhythm, a reaching, sure, effortless cadence which meant endurance.

Such a horse was under him now. His own horse, back in the corrals at Capell, was not to be compared with this one. It couldn't begin to run as this horse ran. Cuyler found himself blessing Paula Juilliard again.

He slowed his pace, twisting in the saddle to listen. Yes, they were back there, pounding after him in pursuit. He could hear the massed rushing of hoofs, not too close, yet close enough. He let his mount out again, working for speed that would hold the pursuit at a distance just too great for shooting. This could very well settle down to a long and deadly chase. His life rode on the cunning with which he nursed his horse's strength.

On either side the night slid by, white and still and peaceful under the stars, with only men and their madness to strike an alien note. Every so often Cuyler would pull down to a jog and listen to the sound of pursuit. That rush of following hoofs was not so loud, now—not because they were any further away but because there were fewer of them. Which meant that some were dropping out back there, either discouraged or because their horses could not hold up to the pace.

Each time Cuyler would hold to this swinging jog, resting his horse, until the thudding hoofs behind would begin creeping a little too close. Then he would lift his horse to a run again, holding his lead, maybe increasing it just a little.

He became aware of a steadily building ache high up on his left arm and of the warm oozing of blood down his arm until the slime of it touched his wrist. He knew the horse would stick to the road without guidance, so now he let the reins run slack while he got out his handkerchief, folded it into a rough pad, reached up inside his shirt and pressed this pad over the wound. He took his neckerchief, wound it around the outside of his shirt to hold the pad in place and knotted it there, setting up on the knot with a pull with his teeth. It was a crude job, but it would help and had to do for the moment.

The chase fled on and the lights of Capell faded to mere pinpricks as the miles drifted back. The next time Cuyler slowed his mount to listen, he felt a jolt of wary surprise. The pound of those pursuing hoofs was closer than at any time before, close and coming fast. Somebody else was riding good horseflesh besides himself, and somebody had played it smart. They had let him set the pace long enough. Now they were setting it. This was the final drive apparently. They were coming full out and he would have to flee full out until something gave, one way or another.

He hadn't played this thing as smart as he figured, after all. What he should have done was, while his horse was fresh, set a blistering pace, gained all the lead he could, then cut away at an angle and perhaps thrown them off the trail, lost them in the night. Instead, thinking only of meeting up with his wagons, he had clung to the Fort Rutledge road. Which had made one thing easy for the pursuit. They could ride full out and not have to slow and puzzle out a trail in the deceptive night. Now, with his horse no longer fresh enough to win back a big lead, those behind were closing in.

This pony of Paula Juilliard's still ran well, but no longer with that free effortlessness. It was working now, and Cuyler, sliding a hand down the side of its neck and across one driving shoulder could feel the wetness of sweat, which was beginning to build up in a roll of foam

78

along the edge of the saddle blanket. Maybe this gallant animal could still outrun the threat coming up from behind. But again, maybe it couldn't.

Cuyler looked back once more. The starlight was a mocking thing. It seemed to disclose, but also it hid. He couldn't see the pursuit, but he could hear it plainer than ever now, even above the pounding stride of his own horse and the rush of wind in his ears.

The exultation of his escape from town was all gone. It had been, after all, just a temporary thing. It was time to think, cold and straight. He couldn't afford another mistake in judgement. If that pursuit kept gaining, kept closing in, there was but one card left to play. Which was to leave his horse in full flight, drop by the road, let the pursuit storm past and then take his chance afoot in the night. Which was risk enough in itself, but not so great a one as to stick stubbornly in the saddle until his mount was run completely into the ground. And he had to make up his mind, quick!

He leaned low, called on his mount for just a little more. The animal responded and the rush of pursuit grew a trifle fainter. If Cuyler was going to leave the saddle, now was the time to do it. He loosened his feet in the stirrups, tried to judge the dark blur of the ground. Then his head jerked up and set his straining senses reaching out once more, this time ahead.

Had it been fact, or fancy buoyed up by

wishful hope and thought? But it seemed that, carrying through the night had come a sound long familiar to his ears. A silvery tinkling, a measured clash, clash and jingle. The song of the yoke bells of a freight outfit.

There—he caught it again! It wasn't fancy—it was fact. Yoke bells singing across the night. Wagons—freight wagons, out there ahead!

Cuyler settled back in his saddle, held his laboring mount to this last closing rush and sent a shout reaching through the night.

'Bill! Bill Wragg!'

'Yo!' came the pealing answer. 'That you, Gene?'

'Right! In trouble, Bill. Send the word back along the wagons. Get everybody up front—with guns. Make it fast!'

Brake blocks squealed as ponderous wagons rolled to a halt. Bill Wragg's voice lifted, harsh and urgent.

'Skeet Yore! Grab your Winchester and get up here! It's Gene, and in trouble. Send the word back!'

Cuyler heard the shouted warning running back from wagon to wagon as he swung his exhausted mount to a stop in the very shadow of the towering bulk of the lead outfit. He dropped from the saddle, drew his gun.

'This way, Bill. Back to meet them!'

He ran back along the road a good hundred yards with Bill Wragg pounding behind him, rifle at ready. The pursuit was still there and coming in fast. But by the sound of it it had thinned out a lot since the start far back at Capell. Probably, Cuyler figured, not over half a dozen riders with horses good enough to last this far. He lifted his six-shooter and sent two quick shots hammering through the night, holding purposefully high, hoping it would halt the onrush, which it did.

'This is Cuyler,' he yelled. 'Take it easy out there. I'm among friends and they're packing Winchesters. Better call things off before somebody gets hurt real bad. Whatever comes will be on your heads if you start it!'

There was some confusion in the pursuit and the rasp and snarl of arguing voices lifted. Cuyler heard his men coming up in back of him, boot heels thudding as they ran.

'Spread out, boys, and get close to the ground,' he called over his shoulder. 'Don't shoot unless I say so. But should it start, make it good!'

These teamsters, these men of the lonely, dusty miles, did not argue or question. They had been with Gene Cuyler for a long time. They were ready to back his hand any time, any place, never questioning his judgment in the slightest.

Out ahead the arguing was still going on. Then Joe Justin's voice lifted clear above the rest.

'He's bluffing, I tell you. What friends would

he find, clear out here? We've run his horse off its feet. We got him cold and he's just stalling for time, trying to run a bluff. We got him. Let's finish this thing—now!'

That did it. They came on in a furious charge. Cuyler, low to the ground, yelled, 'All right, boys—they've asked for it!'

The dark blot of onrushing riders built and grew and Cuyler emptied his gun into the very center of it. On either side of him the rifles of his men tore the night apart in hard, ringing report. And the lead those rifles threw tore the blot of charging riders apart, too. Horses and men crashed down in a wild tangle.

It was almost as if an explosion had taken place, blowing things apart in a dreadful way, shattering and deadly. The remnants of the charge swung wide, dazed and shocked and hurt by the fury of what they had run into. A few scattered shots came flying, high and wild, then some final racing hoofs fading out into the breathless night.

Cuyler called to Bill Wragg and they went ahead cautiously. They found two horses down, and two men. One of the men and both horses were dead. The other rider lay groaning and cursing with the pain of a shattered shoulder. There was no fight left in him.

'Don't cuss us,' Cuyler told him bitterly. 'We didn't start this thing. Your own crowd did.'

'Not cussin' you,' mumbled the wounded man. 'Cussin' that pig-headed fool of a Joe

Justin. He would have it this way. His idea, his and Teede Hunnewell's. We should have listened to Ben Loftus. He never wanted things to go near this far. Who's the other one who went down? I heard him grunt when the slug took him. I hope it's Justin.'

Cuyler scratched a match, leaned over the dead rider. The wounded one twisted around for a look.

'Fell Beasley. Justin got off clean. It would have to be that way. Poor Fell! He didn't ask for any part of this. He just followed along, like the rest of us fools. Damn Joe Justin!'

CHAPTER FIVE

DUSTY WAGONS

The corrals were full of mules, munching hungrily at the feed racks, drinking at dripping troughs, while sleek, yellow-eyed blackbirds fluttered about among them. Men were at work on parked wagons, greasing axles, making repairs here and there after that long trip down from Iron Springs.

Bill Wragg and Skeet Yore had a portable forge set up and going, and were shoeing several mules that stood haltered to the corral fence. Gene Cuyler, a firm bandage about the bullet kiss on his left arm, and favoring the arm only slightly, was helping a couple of other skinners tumble baled hay over the lowered tail gate of one of the wagons.

A buckboard swung out from the lower end of the street and came spinning over to the corrals. Driving it was Ben Loftus. Gene Cuyler climbed down over the hay, mopping the sweat from his face. Ben Loftus sat quietly, his glance swinging here and there, taking in all the activity. Finally he looked at Cuyler.

'Meant it all the time, didn't you?'

'All the time,' Cuyler nodded. 'Something you wanted?'

'My niece's horse and riding rig,' said Loftus.

Cuyler turned to one of his teamsters. 'Zeke, bring out that sorrel bronc I rode last night.' The saddle and other gear were hanging on the corral fence. Cuyler got these and tossed them into the back of Loftus' buckboard.

'I never rode a finer horse than that sorrel,' he said. 'I'll be forever in Miss Juilliard's debt for what she did for me last night.'

'She's a plenty smart girl, that niece of mine is,' observed Loftus, slouching at ease in his buckboard and getting out his pipe.

'Too bad others in these parts haven't got some of her savvy,' said Cuyler drily.

'You probably won't believe this,' Loftus said slowly, 'but I'm glad she warned you last night, glad you got clear and sorry that Hunnewell and Justin forced the issue until smoke had to roll and a pretty good man had to die.'

'Funny talk from you,' Cuyler told him bluntly.

'Sounds that way, for a fact,' Loftus admitted. 'But there's an angle, hard to explain so it's convincing. I never wanted any of this to come to a smoke out, Cuyler. That's the truth, so help me. I've been riding a bluff, all the way. I tried to carry that bluff as far as I could without having things come to any actual shooting. Bluff, and a little manhandling, was enough to discourage those other wagon men. I hoped it might work the same on you. It didn't. So I want you to know now that I'm dragging completely out of the whole argument. Not that I'm afraid of a justified fight, you understand.'

Loftus' glance was level and quiet. Cuyler nodded. 'I can see you're not afraid. But maybe, way deep down, you know you've been wrong all the time and now, with one man dead and another bad hurt, your conscience is kicking over the traces. Right?'

'Call it so,' admitted Loftus. 'It means seeing a lot of good free range slide away from me forever. Yet I can't kick. I've fattened a lot of cows on that range—I've had my use of it. So, I can't rightfully go on denying the same use to other men, even wheat farmers. I'll just have to cut my herd down for lack of grass, that's all.'

'Your idea, or Miss Juilliard's?' asked

Cuyler shrewdly.

Loftus colored slightly. 'Some of both.'

Cuyler spun a smoke into shape, jerked his head. 'How's the grass in those rounded hills, way over there at the east edge of the plains? Any of that country your rightful range?'

'Plenty of it,' said Loftus. 'Plenty of good grass, too, but no water except in winter and early spring. And grass is no good unless there's water to go with it.'

'A thing I never could figure,' said Cuyler, 'is why so many cattlemen can think only in terms of natural water. The wind blows back in those hills, doesn't it?'

'Hell, yes! Of course it does. What's that got to do with it?'

Cuyler pointed to the busy windmill above the corrals.

'That. Half a dozen wells put down in the right places, a mill over each well and a couple of troughs by each mill and there's your water problem in that good grass country whipped for all time. Wheat men aren't interested in those hills and never will be. But cows can graze them just as well as the flats.'

Ben Loftus stared up at the whirring windmill and was silent for some little time. Then he wagged his head and spoke softly, as though slightly bewildered.

'A man gets into the habit of thinking and doing things just one way and he gets so he can't think or do in any other. He gets lock-

86

brained. Cuyler, you've just given me an idea, a hell of a fine idea.'

'Play with it,' said Cuyler. 'Here's another. I think, like I've tried to tell you before, that we can all live and prosper in this country together if we go at it right. You cattlemen, the wheat farmers, and me at my freight hauling. I've hoped from the first to end up friends with everybody and no hard feelings anywhere. To prove that, I'll haul in mills and a drilling rig for you, free of charge and be glad of the chance. It's the only way we can ever lick this thing and keep it sane. Everybody give a little and work together. Think it over, Mr. Loftus, and then pass the idea along to Justin and Hunnewell.'

Ben Loftus' eyes squinted to somberness. 'That,' he said gravely, 'wouldn't do a lick of good. Pass peace talk along to Justin and Hunnewell, I mean. Teede Hunnewell will be out of circulation for some time—you saw to that when you put a slug into his leg. But if I know the man, and I think I do, he'll spend that time figuring how he can get even with you. The only way Hunnewell could ever be brought to behaving himself is to convince him that he hasn't a chance of winning his point. And so far, he's not convinced.'

'From the little I've seen of the two,' Cuyler mused, 'I'd guess that Justin was the tougher of them.'

'And you'd guess right,' Loftus nodded.

'I've known Joe Justin for twenty years, yet, in a way, I don't know him at all. I don't believe anybody really knows Justin except himself. He lives inside himself. Nobody ever sees any part of Justin except the outside layer, and that is tough. What's really underneath, well—your guess is as good as mine. I'm going to hear plenty from him and Hunnewell for drawing out of this trouble.'

'They can't damn you for showing better sense than they do,' commented Cuyler drily.

'But they will. Maybe I'm just lucky—lucky that I've had a family. Maybe a family broadens a man, maybe it softens him. I don't know which. Maybe if I'd been a solitary bachelor like Hunnewell and Justin are, I'd be just as hard to change as they are. But having two girls to chouse me around—well—' Loftus smiled grimly—'that could be the difference.'

'If it is,' grinned Cuyler, 'thank 'em both for me, will you?'

Zeke came up with Paula Juilliard's horse. The sorrel was a trifle gaunt from its hard run of the night before, but was otherwise as good as ever. Its hide shone from a thorough brushing and currying, a chore Cuyler had seen to personally.

With the sorrel tied at lead behind his buckboard, Loftus picked up his reins and kicked off the brake. Again his glance touched Cuyler, sober and level.

'I'm glad the air is cleared between you and

me, Cuyler. I wish I could say the same for Hunnewell and Justin. You got troubles ahead, there. And don't forget this fellow Ivance, who's riding for Justin. He's a bad one to begin with and he won't love you any better for the gun whipping you gave him last night.'

'I know all about Ivance,' said Cuyler. 'We've tangled before, him and me. I helped run him out of the timber country up at Burney. He'll be remembering that, of course, but so will I. That he ran once before when the chips were down. We'll see.'

The buckboard rattled away and Cuyler turned back to his chore of wrestling baled hay. All day long the industry about the corrals went on and when the sun began to lower toward the Brushy Hills in the west, the song of freight bells came down the wind as Mike Kenna brought his wagon rolling back from Sycamore, with the other three outfits following.

Mike climbed down off his wagon, dusty but content.

'Signed, sealed and delivered, Gene,' he grinned. 'Four full loads of wheat. And near two wagonloads of supplies brought back for Gil Saltmarsh. Not a mite of trouble anywhere, except there.' Here Mike's smile faded slightly as he jerked his head toward the third wagon, where Hitch Gower sat the box.

'What sort of trouble, Mike?' asked Cuyler.

'Whiskey. He started liquorin' up in

Sycamore. And he brought a bottle back with him which he's been nippin' at all along the road. I tried to talk him out of it but didn't have any luck. I watched him close and he brought the wagon through all right. But he was growin' pretty rough with the mules toward the last.'

'I'll see what I can do,' Cuyler said.

Hitch Gower was weaving slightly as he climbed down off his wagon. He had a bottle tucked inside his shirt and in his right fist held a short length of chain trace. He started along the line of mules, his bloodshot eyes fixed on one of the near swing animals.

'Just a minute, Gower!' called Cuyler. 'What's on your mind?'

'That damned jughead ain't pulled an ounce all day,' Gower blurted thickly. 'I'm goin' to work it over with this length of chain an' show it damn well who's boss—'

Cuyler grabbed the length of chain, jerked it from Gower's grasp and threw it aside.

'No you don't! Men who run a jerkline for me don't go at a mule that way. A good skinner doesn't have to. And only sober men drive my outfits. Drink all you damn please off duty. But when you're on the job, you stay sober. Remember that in the future.'

Hitch Gower spread his feet to steady himself, glaring at Cuyler, his head swung forward.

'You tryin' to tell me I can't take a shot of

likker whenever I want? Just who do you think you are, anyhow?'

'The man who's paying you wages and who is telling you what you can and can't do while on the job.'

Gower's flushed face twisted into ugliness.

'Right from the first I never liked you, Cuyler. Don't know why I ever sold out to you, or agreed to skin an outfit for you. But I'm damn sure of what I aim to do, right here and now!'

With the words, Gower hunched his shoulders forward and aimed a punch at Cuyler's face. It was the slowed, pawing, clumsy punch of a drunken man. Cuyler avoided the blow easily and Gower, carried forward by his empty effort, fell to his hands and knees. The whiskey bottle dropped from his open shirt front.

Gene Cuyler caught up the bottle and smashed it against the iron tire of a wagon wheel.

'You're through, Gower,' he rapped curtly. 'You got two days' wages coming and here they are. Take 'em and get out!'

Gower, lurching to his feet, tried to knock the money from Cuyler's hand. But Cuyler grabbed him, jammed the money into his pocket, spun him around and gave him a shove.

'Get out!'

Mumbling and cursing, Gower stumbled

off, calling obscenities back over his shoulder. Mingled with these was clumsy threat.

'You ain't seen the last of me, Cuyler. I'll get even—!'

The slim, precise, immaculate figure of Pierce Pomeroy, coming down from town, stepped aside and watched Hitch Gower pass, with an expression of open distaste. Then the banker turned and came on over to the wagons.

'Thought I'd drop around and see how things were shaping up, Cuyler,' Pomeroy said. 'Trouble, maybe—with him?' He nodded toward the departing Gower.

Cuyler explained and Pomeroy shrugged.

'Good riddance. Too much money tied up in an outfit to entrust it to a drunk.'

Cuyler showed the banker around and explained the improvements he intended making in the way of rejuvenating the old adobe building and in enlarging the corrals and other needed facilities.

'I've been looking into things,' said Pomeroy. 'I understand that there is an heir to this property running loose somewhere, but the property is badly tax delinquent. Chances are I can manage to force things to a tax sale. If so, I'll let you know and you'll be able to pick it up for a song. The cattle crowd gave you another bad time last night, didn't they?'

'Pretty bad,' Cuyler admitted. 'I was sorry to see it come to a smoke rolling, but they would have it that way. One good thing came out of it. Ben Loftus and I have smoked the peace pipe. There'll be no more trouble for me with the J L outfit. I'm hoping the idea will be taking, with some of the other cow layouts.'

'Loftus,' said Pomeroy, with a little click of his teeth, 'knows which side his bread is buttered on. And he'd better!'

Which was a startling remark, but before Cuyler could ask for an elaboration of it, the banker had turned away and was moving off.

Cuyler ordered the two wagons loaded with supplies up to Gil Saltmarsh's store and rode up on one of them to help unload. Steve Sears, his old self again, rode with him. Gil Saltmarsh greeted them with a wide grin.

'This is something like. The store was gettin' so damned empty it was turnin' spooky.'

It was pleasant, working there in the first blue sundown shadows, thought Gene Cuyler. Good to heft a fifty pound sack of flour on your sound shoulder and lug it into the store. Good to be young, to do the job at hand and look forward to all the other jobs of the future. Good to have a lusty, faithful, hard-fighting and hard-working crew behind you. Like the men who had brought his wagons down from Iron Springs. Like Mike Kenna yonder and young Steve Sears out front, muscling supplies down from the wagons and whistling cheerfully as he toiled.

And particularly good to know that from

93

here on out there'd be no more trouble with Ben Loftus and his outfit. This fact was a big step ahead toward the eventual conditions of peace and amicability Cuyler had hoped for. Maybe Loftus' sober predictions about Teede Hunnewell's and Joe Justin's future actions had been overly gloomy. Maybe these two, minus Loftus' support, would give the whole argument up as a bad job and leave well enough alone. It wouldn't cost anything to hope so, anyhow.

Hoofs pattered in the street dust and it was Candy Loftus who came riding into town, heading for the store. She pulled even with the wagons, reined in to stare at them with hostile blue eyes. Steve Sears, straightening up from his labors, saw her and grinned.

'Hello, there!' he called boyishly.

Candy froze him with a glance, reined past the wagons and swung in to a hitch rail. That was when a pair of mongrel dogs who had been prowling the streets and bristling at each other all day, decided to have it out. And the spot they picked for a showdown was right under the very nose of Candy's mount.

It had always been part of Candy Loftus' hard-riding, helter-skelter, heedless flair for life to ride the most spirited and skittish animals her father would allow. And sometimes, when her father wasn't around at the moment, to pick one even wilder than usual. Like this one she was up on now and which, with a tangle of

94

yelping, snarling dogs abruptly beginning to unwind right under its very feet, went high into the air and came down pitching.

All of which wouldn't have worried Candy in the slightest, had she been fully settled in the saddle. But at this moment she had been about to step down and the first spinning lunge of her horse threw her forward and to one side. As she fell, Candy made a wild grab for the saddle horn and barely managed to get hold of it with one hand.

There she hung, far down along the horse's side, her foot twisted in the stirrup and the animal pitching wildly. Candy couldn't pull back into the saddle and the twisting wind of the bucking horse kept her from kicking free of the stirrup. If she let go of the saddle horn it meant at the very least a bad fall, and at the worst, with her foot tangled in the stirrup, it meant being dragged and maybe kicked to death.

Candy realized all this in sudden, terrified reality. This was bad! And she knew she couldn't hold on to the saddle horn much longer. Already her desperately set fingers were growing numb while her arm felt as if it was being jerked from its socket—!

Gene Cuyler, just coming out of the store after another sack of flour, saw and measured the desperation of this slim, heedless, yellow-haired girl's predicament and he vaulted the hitch rail, intent on grabbing the horse, if possible. But Steve Sears was there ahead of him.

Steve left the wagon in one long leap, flashed in on the pitching horse, grabbed the trailing reins with one hand and managed to wrap his free arm about Candy Loftus' dangling figure. Steve had a mad scramble on his hands for a moment before Cuyler, dodging a flailing hoof, leaped at the horse's head, got a handful of reins close up to the bridle bit, set his heels and dragged the horse's head around and back, cramping it until the animal almost fell.

This anchored the horse long enough for Steve Sears to flip Candy Loftus' foot free and dodge into the clear with Candy in his arms. The horse, under the stern authority of Cuyler's grip, quickly quieted. The cause of the whole affair, the dog fight, was already over, with the vanquished fleeing at the top of its lungs, the victor whooping triumph a scant yard behind.

Steve Sears set Candy Loftus on her feet and grinned down at her.

'Little girls like you shouldn't ride such frisky broncs. You came mighty close to getting some dust on that pretty nose.'

It took Candy a moment to get her scattered wits together and regain some remnant of her shaken dignity. She glared at Steve.

'You didn't have to b-butt in, wagon man. I was doing all right.'

Steve laughed cheerfully.

'Not from where I sat, you weren't. That was the darnedest way to try and ride a pitching bronc I ever saw. Anyway, you're all safely in one piece and not too badly mussed up. You're Candy Loftus, of course? I'm Steve Sears.'

'And I,' said Candy icily, 'am not in the least interested in who you are.'

She brushed Steve's steadying arm aside, walked over and tried to take the rein of her now-quieted horse from Gene Cuyler, who refused to relinquish it, but led the horse to the hitch rail and tied it there.

Steve Sears stared after Candy ruefully, his cheery grin fading somewhat. Then he shrugged and climbed back into the wagon.

Candy tried again to get hold of her horse.

'I can tie my own pony,' she said stiffly. 'And prefer to.'

Gene Cuyler's voice was low and curt.

'You are the most completely obnoxious person I ever ran across, Candy Loftus. Here that fine kid, Steve Sears, definitely saved your silly little neck from being badly bent, if not broken, which you know full well. Yet you aren't even good enough sport to thank him. Instead you try and act uppity. Spoiled, selfish—the poorest sport in the world. That's you!'

Gene was angry, plenty, and under the whiplash cut of his tone and words, Candy Loftus flushed.

'I—I don't like wagon men,' she defended

97

somewhat lamely.

'And wagon men don't like you,' Gene shot back. 'I wonder that anybody does.'

He turned and went back to his work.

Candy had come to town to get some sort of sewing trinkets. Now, for all her swagger and arrogance, she somehow lacked the courage to go into the store. She was far more shaken than she cared to admit.

She fussed a bit over the reins, getting them free, preparing to mount. While doing so she darted a couple of swift glances at Steve Sears, who was now bent over his job and paying her no attention at all. Which fact left Candy with a queer and biting disappointment. She swung astride her chastened pony, reined wide of the wagons and headed for home. Even now, as she went, Steve Sears seemed to have forgotten her existence completely.

*   *   *

For the next three weeks Gene Cuyler had time and thought for nothing else but long hours of grinding, endless toil. His men had repaired the damaged wagon. On this job, Luke Malcolm had shown such an aptitude with tools Cuyler decided to start him on the chore of enlarging and repairing corrals and feed sheds and making a check of the old adobe building so that they would have some idea of what was necessary in bringing it back to usefulness.

All of which, short one skinner now after firing Hitch Gower, made it necessary for Gene to take over a jerkline of one outfit himself. So the days and nights saw him rolling out the dusty miles, back and forth, from the Vaca Plains to Sycamore, out there beyond the Brushy Hills.

With six double rigs and five single ones, seventeen big Merivale wagons in all, Jim Nickerson and the other wheat ranchers were joyous over the way their storing barns were beginning to empty. They began laying plans for plowing and sowing bigger acreages the following year and eagerly estimated the current harvest, which would start before too long, what with the wheat beginning to turn from green to tawny, ripening in the big fields.

Not a hint of trouble had shown since the shootout along the Fort Rutledge road, but grizzled old Bill Wragg, drawing on the wisdom of a lifetime among violent men and their ways, spoke with blunt caution.

'A wolf is always quietest when he's up to some sort of hell raisin'. He may lift his howl before and after, but he's quiet when goin' in for a kill. Take nothin' for granted, Gene.'

They made an impressive sight, those seventeen wagons with their long strings of mules, rolling in a ponderous snake of movement. The chime of the leaders' yoke bells filled canyon and draw across the Brushies with shimmering music and the dust rolled up in a great long banner which, at a distance, was powdered gold in the sun. Up on the wagon boxes, however, this dust was something to peer through, to swear at but stoically endure. For it was a part of the game, a badge of the trade, of dusty men and dusty mules and dusty wagons.

Sycamore was a little drowsy town, on the west bank of the Sarco River, where fresh water and tide water met at a wide basin where the little river steamers turned. Fifty miles south and west, the Sarco River opened into San Francisco Bay, where the clipper ships waited to fill their holds with this same Vaca Plains wheat and then take to the high seas with this food for a hungry world. For some of these tall ships the Orient was the goal; for others it was the long, perilous trace around the Horn.

The heyday of California's outpouring of metallic gold was over; the high gulches and flats of the Sierra Nevada gold camps no longer the central topic and goal of all men. Now it was wheat, a new treasure of the soil that this sunset land was pouring out.

Just above the turning basin the road crossed the Sarco River by means of a cavernous, covered bridge, which smelled of cobwebs and dust and shadowed heat and which boomed thunderously to the measured tramp of the mules and the rumble of wagon wheels. Myriads of barn swallows had their nests of mud daub up under the eaves and in the dusky rafters and they swarmed and twittered in and out each time the wagons crossed.

The river boats berthed at the lower end of town and here were wooden chutes, worn slick and shiny with use, down which the sacked wheat slid from wagon bed to cargo deck. The majority of the wagons rolled empty on the return trip to Capell, but some carried consignments of freight and supplies of one sort or another, harvesting and other farm equipment for the wheat ranchers, staples for Gil Saltmarsh's store.

One day there were crated windmills, pumps and pipe and heavy timbers for the towers. And there was a drill rig. As they loaded this, Gene Cuyler turned to Steve Sears.

'This means that Ben Loftus is going after water in those foothills east of the plains, kid. You and me'll haul this stuff out to the J L tomorrow.'

The road to the J L headquarters ran east from Capell, skirting one of Jim Nickerson's big fields, breaking into open and unfenced plains country beyond, where cattle grazed and drifted or gathered to rest in the shade of great, spreading valley oak trees. In the far distance, where several of these big oaks clustered, the ranch building shone white. With Gene Cuyler at the jerkline and Steve Sears whistling on the box beside him, the double-wagon outfit rolled

101

on through the morning sunlight, cutting down the miles slowly but surely.

Steve's whistle broke off and he said abruptly, 'You can't beat the land, Gene. Not too many years ago this stretch of country was a wilderness, giving nothing to the world. But the land was there, waiting, waiting to give, once men got ready to work with it. Other things come and go, but the land is always there.'

Cuyler looked at him, grinned. 'Kid, you surprise me. Never thought you had any more on your mind than today and tomorrow and a chance to whistle. You've grown up on me. Next thing you'll be figuring on gettin' married and raisin' a family.'

Steve flushed slightly, then chuckled. 'If I am, it's your fault. You started me savin' my money.'

Cuyler was glad of this chance to pay a legitimate visit to the J L headquarters. For, since that deadly night on the hotel porch, he had neither seen nor heard anything of Paula Juilliard. And he had thought of her a lot, remembering many little things that were strangely good to remember.

The silken shine of her sleek, dark head and the way she carried it, proud and erect. The quick, lithe grace with which she moved, the sound of her voice and the memory of her standing close to him, there in the pocket of darkness close to the hotel wall, while stark danger trod the street of Capell under the white stars.

The emotion that was in her, her stammered words as to why she had ridden to warn him, the beat of her clenched fists against his chest in her anxiety over the portent of danger. And finally, the delicate perfume of her hair, disordered by her wild ride.

All these things had Gene Cuyler remembered and gone over again and again, locked in his thoughts while his wagons had rolled out the slow, dusty miles across the Brushies. Now, as the ranch headquarters loomed closer and closer, a lifting eagerness was running all through him, eagerness for the sight of her again and for the sound of her voice.

Steve Sears broke in on Gene's thoughts with another chuckling remark.

'Looks peaceful enough from here, but I wouldn't be a mite surprised to have that yellow-headed little rascal of a Candy Loftus jump up out of a ditch somewhere and start throwing rocks at us. Long as her pa has smoked the peace pipe with us, you'd think maybe she'd be ready to tolerate us, too.'

'That young lady,' said Cuyler, 'is about as perverse and ornery as any I ever ran across in my time. She's a spoiled, selfish, arrogant little hoyden, and her pa made the mistake of his life in not wearing out an armful of switches on her every other day or so.'

'She's pretty,' said Steve slowly. 'Pretty as a sunbeam—and probably twice as hard to corral.'

Cuyler smiled. 'So's a nest of bob-cats. The man who wins that young lady's favor is going to have to show her just who's boss—and plenty! Otherwise she'll sure lead him a merry race down the misery trail. Ha! Speak of the little devil and there she is!'

Sure enough it was Candy, coming in from some errand out on the range and coming at top speed, her pony stretched out at a full gallop, her yellow hair flying.

'She can ride!' exclaimed Steve, his eyes shining. 'Look at her go, will you!'

Candy flashed through the mottled shade of the oaks, left her saddle with an agile leap and went into the ranchhouse, her head high, her step jaunty.

'Just to show how little we amount to in her young opinion,' drawled Cuyler. 'She's throwing rocks, Steve—but not the kind you pick up off the ground.'

The road forked, the left branch running straight up to the ranchhouse, the right cutting around the oaks to the corrals beyond. Cuyler brought the wagons to a stop, went up to the ranchhouse and knocked. Paula Juilliard opened the door.

She was in starched gingham and held a dusting cloth in one hand. Sight of her sent Gene Cuyler's pulses to singing. He pulled off his hat.

'Morning, Miss Juilliard. Mr. Loftus around? I got his windmills and drill rig out there.'

'You should find Uncle Ben out around the corrals somewhere,' she told him.

They stood for a moment, looking at each other. The girl's eyes fell and warm color crept up her slim throat.

'This is the first chance I've had to thank you for the warning you brought me,' said Cuyler, 'and for the loan of that swell sorrel horse. I'll never be out of debt to you.'

'As long as things turned out as well as they did, I'm happy,' she said simply. 'And it served to bring Uncle Ben fully to his senses. But he isn't the only one. You must be careful and ever on the watch.'

'You're a grand girl, Paula,' said Cuyler.

The touch of color in her throat flushed slightly.

'Thanks, Gene.' She flashed a smile, whisked away and was gone.

Cuyler went back to the wagons and as he climbed up to the box, Steve Sears grinned and said, 'You'd think the man was climbing over clouds, with little pink angels fluttering round about like butterflys over a sweet-clover field.'

'You,' growled Cuyler, 'shut up! Else I'll chuck you off this wagon on top of your silly head.'

Steve chuckled, drummed his heels against

the wagon side and broke out whistling again.

Ben Loftus was at the corrals and he came up to the wagons eagerly.

'I've been like a kid waiting for Christmas. Once you sold me the idea I couldn't wait to try it out. I wrote in, ordering that gear, that very same day. We'll unload it over there at that shed.'

'Why not let us haul it right out to the spots you intend to drill?' offered Cuyler. 'Then one unloading will do the job.'

'You're being mighty damn fair, Cuyler,' said Loftus. 'I'll get some of the boys to give a hand. That stuff looks heavy.'

Among others in the hands that Loftus called up were Blaze Doan and Cass Huntoon. They were at no pains to hide the dislike they felt. Cass Huntoon was openly antagonistic, while Blaze Doan wore a constant, covert sneer. It was plain, Cuyler thought, that though Ben Loftus was thoroughly friendly at last, this feeling did not extend to some of his crew.

'We're doin' 'em a favor,' murmured Steve Sears, 'and they hate our innards. That Blaze Doan, I'd sure like to have a little private ruckus with him. Just him and me, with plenty of room round about and nobody to interfere. I'd knock that sneer off his face.'

'Mind your lip and your step,' ordered Gene quietly. 'Doan and Huntoon are the only soreheads. The rest are decent enough.'

106

Ben Loftus wasn't blind to the attitude of Doan and Huntoon and Cuyler saw him draw them aside and lay some stern words on them. After which they were sulky, but they watched their step. So the spotting of the material and the unloading of it went through without incident.

Ben Loftus rode the wagons back to the corrals and said, just before dropping off, 'When I hit the first water, get a mill up and actually pumping, I'll let you know, Cuyler, so you can come out and see for yourself. It was your idea and you'll probably get a lift out of seeing it working.'

It was mid-afternoon by this time and as Gene Cuyler and Steve Sears rolled the empty wagons past the road forks, Gene looked over at the house. A buckboard stood in front of it and in the shade of the porch two people were sitting and talking. One was Paula Juilliard. The other was Pierce Pomeroy, the banker.

For no reason that made sense at all, the day seemed suddenly less warm and bright to Gene Cuyler. He was silent and grave of face, all the way back to town.

CHAPTER SIX

CANYON TRAGEDY

That evening things were pretty quiet about the freight corrals, what with all the other outfits being down to Sycamore with another consignment of wheat. So, with the chores cleaned up, Gene Cuyler and Steve Sears wandered up town and stopped in at Gil Saltmarsh's store. The place was brightly lighted and showed no sign of closing up. Cuyler remarked about this.

'You've been so busy you've lost count of the days,' the storekeeper answered. 'This happens to be Saturday night and I always keep open pretty late, so's to take care of some of the little, faraway outfits who seldom get into town at any other time. Then again, tonight is jig night, which always brings in a little extra trade.'

'Jig night! You mean there's goin' to be a dance?' asked Steve Sears eagerly.

Saltmarsh nodded.

'That's what. Odd Fellows' Hall. Every month they have one. But I wouldn't figure on being particularly welcome there, young feller. These dances are pretty much a cow folk party, though town people are in on it, too.'

'Ain't been to a jig in a coon's age,' said

Steve. 'I'd sure like to flip a heel again. Why shouldn't I go? I can be as regular a gent as the next one.'

'Sure you can,' agreed Saltmarsh drily. 'But that ain't the point. The point is, you're a wagon man. Which makes a difference with some who'll be present.'

Steve turned to Cuyler. 'What do you think, Boss?'

'It might all depend on who you asked to dance with you,' Cuyler observed, with a sly depth of meaning. 'I doubt if *she* would, even if you asked her real pretty.'

Steve colored hotly.

'I can at least ask her. Shucks! I'm free, white and twenty-one. I ain't murdered anybody, or robbed any banks or stole any horses. I got a good notion to get slicked up and take in that jig.'

'Go ahead,' Cuyler grinned. 'They can't do much worse than chuck you out on your neck.'

By the time Steve got back from slicking up, the street was livening. Riders were drifting in and buckboards were whirling past the store. The Odd Fellows' Hall was across the street and about halfway along toward the hotel. It was aglow with light and a group was already forming about the open door. More hoofs rattled and two horses turned in to the hitch rail in front of the store. It was Candy Loftus who came in squired by Blaze Doan.

Candy was a picture. She had on a divided

109

skirt of golden yellow corduroy and a silk blouse of the same color. These, along with her bared, yellow head, brushed to shining luxury now, put a sort of glow about her and Steve Sears, mightily impressed before, now went completely under. His shining, eager eyes followed her as though drawn by a magnet, a fact which Blaze Doan did not miss and which brought a scowl to Doan's face.

Candy paid Steve and Cuyler not the slightest visible notice as she dickered with Gil Saltmarsh over a new scarf to add to her outfit. Her eyes and cheeks were bright and glowing, her laughter high and light and careless. Altogether she was as colorful, and impudent and provocative a little baggage as Gene Cuyler had ever seen.

When she went out, holding Blaze Doan's arm and laughing up at him, Cuyler flashed a look at Steve Sears and almost winced at the look on his face. Steve was gone, head over heels, and Cuyler couldn't see anything ahead of the kid in this affair but misery. He knew he couldn't head it off, but he tried.

'Let's go over to the hotel and forget the whole thing, Steve.'

Steve shook a stubborn head.

'I'm goin' to that jig and I'm goin' to dance with her.' He went out, into the night.

Cuyler hung around the store a while longer, then started back to the hotel. He passed the Odd Fellows' Hall on the far side of the street

110

as a matter of plain common sense. There would be a preponderantly cattle crowd grouped about the door of the hall and there was no percentage in challenging unnecessary trouble. Things had quieted down across the plains, so he'd been able to get in three good weeks of solid work. It was a condition of things which he wanted to see continue.

Yet, he was young, and not above being a little lonely on such a night as this. Which was why he had not tried to dissuade Steve Sears too strongly. He could understand and sympathize with Steve's youth.

He paused in a blot of shadow under an oak tree, to watch the crowd and listen to the jocular gayness of men's voices and the happy laughter of the women folks. He was building a cigarette when a buckboard came whirling down street, then swung in to an empty place at a hitch rail. Two people got down and crossed to the hall. As they came into the light flare from the door, Cuyler's fingers, busy with brown paper and tobacco, went still.

Paula Juilliard and Pierce Pomeroy.

Cuyler watched them go in, mingling with the cheerful crowd. The cigarette in his fingers crumpled to bits of tobacco and torn paper. He swung abruptly about and crossed over to the hotel, where Sam Reeves was at the table in the lobby, setting out the chessboard.

'Don't believe your chess partner will show up tonight, Sam,' said Cuyler. 'I just saw him going to the dance.'

'Doggone!' wailed Reeves. 'I forgot all about that jig. Who's Pierce squiring? Paula Juilliard, I suppose. I know he's plenty fond of her.'

Cuyler's face was inscrutable.

'I'll give you a whirl at that game. I've played it a few times.'

'The deuce! Why didn't you say so, long time ago? Sit down, man—sit down!'

Sam Reeves won the first game in short order and chortled in his triumph. But the second game found the going a lot tougher, as Cuyler began to get the feel of things again. The hotel was warmly quiet, but over at the hall the music had started and the strains of it carried in faintly.

Sam Reeves might have been listening to that music. At any rate he left his queen wide open and Gene collared it. Sam scratched his head ruefully as he scanned the setup.

'No need playin' this one out. Sure looked kinda bad there. Which makes it game and game. How about a rubber?'

Gene Cuyler nodded. Matters settled down to dogged fencing. The best part of an hour drifted by without any particular advantage gained by either of them. Then, abruptly into their concentration broke an uproar out in the street, and as Cuyler jerked his head up to listen, a single, shrill yell carried clearly.

'Fight—!'

Premonition hit Cuyler as he ran out into the street. The ruckus was in front of the Hall, a pushing, milling group of men, with more streaming from the Hall all the time. Cuyler drove toward the center of things, using his elbows and the weight of his big shoulders.

He heard a man say, 'Blaze Doan and one of the damn mule skinners!'

Cuyler swore silently. His fault as much as anyone's. He shouldn't have let Steve Sears take in this jig. He might have known something like this would be the inevitable result.

Throwing the full weight and power of his shoulders into the drive, and followed by the muttered curses of those he elbowed aside, Cuyler finally broke through the crowd. There in front of him was the dark tangle of the two fighters. Sounded grunts, hard panting breath, and the smack and thump of blows.

Cuyler made no move to interfere. This was between Steve and Doan. Steve would either whip his man or take a licking himself. Either way, no great harm would be done so long as the row did not stir up something that could not be stopped. The crowd was openly partisan, whooping encouragement to Blaze Doan.

The crowd swayed back and forth, following the give and take of the fighters. One of the tangled figures seemed to trip and almost go down, an advantage his opponent was quick to

113

capitalize on, leaping to the attack with hammering blows. A deep, angry voice called out of the crowd.

'Don't try that again, Huntoon! Maybe the kid is a wagon man, but he's been making a fair fight of this and he's got a right to a fair shake in return. You trip him again and I'll punch your ugly face in!'

So Steve was the one who was taking it heavily now, with Blaze Doan swarming all over him, and because Cass Huntoon had tripped Steve treacherously! Anger leaped in Gene Cuyler, whipping along his nerve ends, knotting his fists. He drove around the circle of the crowd, trying to identify Huntoon in the tricky dark. As he went he lifted an encouraging yell.

'Stay with him, Steve! Stay with him, kid!'

Cuyler couldn't find Huntoon, but that yell which made Steve realize he had at least one friend in this crowd, lifted him up and sent him back into the fray with new fury. For a moment it was raw give and take. Then movement started as one of the fighters began backing up and kept on backing up. This movement carried the battlers into the light of the hall door and a growl of dismay went through the partisan crowd. For it was Blaze Doan who was backing up and it was Steve Sears who was pouring it on.

Steve's hat was gone, his curly hair tangled. A dark smear of blood ran down over his

114

mouth and chin, but Steve was carrying the fight to his taller, rangier opponent with a fiery gusto that warmed Gene Cuyler's heart. Again he yelled.

'You got him going, kid—stay with him!'

A rumble of anger lifted from those close about Cuyler, but this was wiped out as Steve nailed the weakening Doan squarely on the jaw with a right hand which started from way back and which spat like a splitting board when it landed.

Blaze Doan went down and stayed there.

Somebody in the crowd took a swipe at Steve but missed him. Cuyler made a dive for the fellow, caught him trying to duck away and knocked him flat with a wicked smash. Then it was Ben Loftus bursting angrily through the crowd and taking a place in front of panting, bloody Steve.

'Lay off this kid!' he yelled. 'It was a fair fight and we keep it so. Blaze Doan asked for it and he got it. This kid licked him, fair and square. Anybody who takes another sneak punch at Sears has got me to lick. Now get back to your dancing. The fight's over!'

The crowd milled about, still sullen. The fellow Gene Cuyler had knocked down was helped up and away by some friends. It was Ben Loftus who grabbed Blaze Doan by the neck and hauled him to his feet, where Doan stood weaving and wobbly, barely able to stand.

115

'I warned you, Doan,' rapped the irate cattleman. 'I told you what to expect if you went out of your way to start trouble with Cuyler or any of his men. I aim to keep my word. Now get out of here!'

He gave Doan a shove and the beaten puncher went stumbling off, with Ben Loftus, still bristling, following at his heels. Gene Cuyler took hold of Steve.

'Come on over to the hotel, kid.'

Steve came along docilely enough and when Cuyler got him to his room, Steve was grinning through puffed and battered lips.

'I danced with her, Gene,' he mumbled triumphantly. 'It was a Dan Tucker and Blaze Doan was whistlin' the changes. I got into the dance with a biscuit shooter from the Elite Café and then, when the grand right and left brought Candy up to me, I whistled. Before she could even think twice I was dancing with her. Doan came barging right over and took a swing at me. So I invited him to step outside and cut his wolf loose. Yes, sir! I danced with Candy Loftus. She's—she's—!' Steve just seemed unable to find words to express it, but by the glow in his eyes, both of which were rapidly turning black and purple and one of them already swollen almost shut, it was plain that he thought Candy Loftus nothing short of wonderful.

'Huh!' grunted Gene drily. 'So you danced with her. And like to got the waddin' punched out of you. Think it was all worth the price?'

'If Blaze Doan had broke me in half it would still have been worth it,' enthused Steve. 'But I licked him. And danced with Candy. She's marvelous!'

'All right, so you think she's marvelous. Well, you're a mess. Get that shirt off. You've been spouting gore all over it like a wounded buffalo. Hit that water jug and basin and go to scrubbing. I'll loan you a clean shirt. But get this. Candy Loftus has no more use for a wagon man than she has for a rattlesnake. She'll bring you nothin' but misery and trouble. You've had your little dream. Now wake up!'

'Rats!' Steve mumbled, through the shirt he was dragging over his head. 'You sound like a sour old coot who don't understand such things. That girl will like me a lot before I'm through.'

Washed clean and with a fresh shirt on, Steve was all for heading back to the dance until he got a look at himself in the glass above the bureau. Sight of his puffed lips, his black eyes with the one now swollen completely shut, along with sundry other swellings, bruises, scrapes and cuts, forced him to ruefully admit he wasn't in the best of shape to excite feminine admiration.

'Likewise,' Gene reminded him, 'you'll be stiff and sore as a boil tomorrow morning, with plenty of work coming up. Best thing you can do is hit the hay.'

To which Steve soberly agreed.

Gene Cuyler went back to the hotel lobby to see none other than Miss Candy Loftus herself standing beside the door, pouting and glowering. At Gene's glance she tossed her head. Gene grinned.

'Steve says to thank you for the dance, Candy. And he's sorry it couldn't have lasted longer.'

'I hope I never see him again,' flared Candy. 'He spoiled my evening and he got Blaze Doan fired. I hate him! You can tell him that for me.'

'He wouldn't believe it if I did. And I don't think you do. You danced with him, remember.'

'I—I couldn't help myself,' Candy sputtered furiously. 'He had hold of me before I knew it.'

'What are you doing here? I can still hear music going on.'

Candy turned her back on him without answering. But Gene understood a moment later when Ben Loftus and Paula Juilliard came in.

Loftus spoke sternly. 'All right, Candy. We're going home, now! Come along.'

Candy marched out, her small spine ramrod stiff.

Cuyler said, 'I'm sorry about this, Mr. Loftus. Steve meant no harm. He's a good kid.'

'I'm not blaming Sears,' growled Loftus. 'Of course he meant no harm. But that cussed fool of a Blaze Doan, taking a swing at Sears just because the kid whistled a change in the dance so he could whirl Candy a couple of times—! Anybody would think Doan figured he owned Candy. I damn well showed him different. I fired him. Fired Cass Huntoon, too. I've had a big plenty of the pair of them.'

'I'll be along just as soon as Pierce brings the buckboard, Uncle Ben,' said Paula Juilliard.

'I know,' nodded Loftus. 'I never did have to worry a minute about you, Paula. But that Candy—!' He hurried out.

Cuyler looked at Paula, grave and still and lovely in her blue party dress, a white silk scarf thrown over her shoulders.

'Why didn't you come to the dance, Gene? I was hoping you would.'

'And would you have danced with me?'

She nodded her dark head, a smile on her lips. Gene took a step toward her, but stopped as Pierce Pomeroy came in.

The banker said, 'All ready, Paula.'

Pomeroy looked at Gene, his black eyes unreadable. But his tone was hard and crisp when he spoke.

'If you expect to win and hold the goodwill of folks around here, Cuyler, you'll see to it that in the future neither you or any of your men start trouble. Tonight's affair was inexcusable. It might be a good idea to fire young Sears.'

Cuyler met the banker's glance for a full,

long second. He shook his head.

'Couldn't think of it. Steve's a good boy.'

'I'm still telling you to fire him,' snapped Pomeroy.

Cuyler's jaw tightened. 'Aren't you getting a little off the trail, Pomeroy? My men stick by me, I stick by them. I know how to run my outfits.'

Pomeroy's black eyes were hard as glass and you couldn't see a millionth part of an inch into them. 'Your outfits?' he purred. 'You're sure of that?'

The frost gathered in Cuyler's glance, but he held his temper under tight rein. 'I don't understand this heavy club all of a sudden, Pomeroy,' he said quietly. 'Just why you should rile up over something that was strictly between Steve and Blaze Doan, I can't figure. Ben Loftus just admitted that it was Doan's fault. He isn't blaming Steve at all, so why should you?'

Paula Juilliard was looking from one to the other of these two men. She spoke hurriedly.

'Of course it was Blaze Doan's fault, Pierce. I saw it all. As Gene says, it didn't really amount to a hill of beans, anyway. There have been fights at these Saturday night dances before and no permanent harm done. Come, I want to get along home.'

There was dark blood burning in Pierce Pomeroy's face and his lips were twisted for angry retort. But he got a grip on himself and

120

put out his arm.

'All right, Paula.'

Gene Cuyler waited until the last sound of the buckboard dwindled out in the night, then went slowly to his room, his face hard and thoughtful.

* * *

The next morning, leaving Steve to care for odd jobs about the corrals, Gene Cuyler saddled up his horse and rode all down through the wheat country. The past few weeks had brought the new crop along fast. No longer were the fields vast spreads of rippling green. Now they were taking on a tawny, golden brown look and the heads were heavy and fat. Machines were mowing and raking up several swathes of grain along every line fence. Following along behind were teams of heavy work horses, pulling gang plows and turning up several furrows of reddish brown earth. With the wheat ripening and turning dry enough to burn readily, the ranchers were taking all possible precautions against fire, whether it start by accident or design on the part of hostile cattle interests.

On his way back to town Cuyler stopped in for a chat with Jim Nickerson and presently spoke of the activity of the mowers and plows along the line fences.

'I see you're taking no chances on fire, Jim.'

Nickerson shrugged. 'A man learns as he goes along. I want no cowpoke happening by, flipping a match into the edge of my wheat. It's been tried before and some people can sure hang on to an idea.'

'You've no need to worry about the J L outfit any more,' said Cuyler. He went on to tell of the peace pact with Ben Loftus.

'That's the best of news,' exclaimed Nickerson in hearty satisfaction. 'If Loftus gave his word, he'll keep it. As for Teede Hunnewell and Joe Justin, I don't know. They're pretty quiet now and I'd like to believe they've decided to call quits. But I don't think they have. My hunch is they're waiting for Hunnewell to be up and around again before starting more trouble.'

Riding back through town, Cuyler saw a burly figure lounging along the street. It was Hitch Gower, the skinner he'd had to fire. It was the first he'd seen of Gower since that day, and he wondered idly what was keeping Gower around Capell, unless it was the intention of getting even, as he had threatened to do. Gower threw a surly glance as Cuyler rode by, but made no comment or hostile move.

His chores about the corrals caught up, Steve Sears was basking in the sun. He grinned wrily at Cuyler.

'You were right, mister. I'm plenty stiff and sore. I must have stopped more than I thought, last night. Are you quite sure Doan wasn't using a club on me? How do I look?'

'Kind of lopsided in spots,' Cuyler drawled. 'I don't know when I ever saw a better pair of shiners.'

Steve fingered an eye gently. 'Saw an old friend of yours when I went up town for a bite of grub. Hitch Gower. He was just coming out of the bank. I thought he'd left town.'

'So did I.' Cuyler nodded. 'I saw him just now, myself. Let him be an example to you, my bumptious young friend. Always be boss of your liquor.'

'Huh!' grunted Steve, 'liquor never did bother me. But that Candy Loftus sure has got me fightin' my head. She's a darlin'.'

'A little devil, you mean,' corrected Cuyler, chuckling. 'And an ornery little one, with thorns all over her. I told you she'd bring you nothin' but misery.'

When the wagons came rolling in from Sycamore just at sundown, there was a leathery, silent skinner, one Tim Stout, riding with Mike Kenna.

'Here's a good man, looking for a job, Gene,' said Mike. 'I told him I thought you could use him.'

'Swell!' exclaimed Gene. 'I sure can. This means I can let go of that jerkline for a while and tend to other items of business, of which there are plenty piling up. Glad to have you with us, Stout. Your pay starts right now.'

Later, Gene asked Mike Kenna how the

123

other wagon men were doing around Sycamore, if they were finding any hauling to do.

'They're not doing too well,' Mike answered soberly. 'In fact, most of them are doin' nothin' at all. They're camped out along the river and feelin' pretty low. Which I hate to see, for they're mostly old friends of mine.'

'Who among them would you recommend as being particularly long-headed and dependable?'

Mike considered a moment. 'Jess Petty is a good man.'

'I'll see him. I'm heading for Sycamore this evening. Keep rolling that wheat out, Mike. I was down through the ranches today and the crop coming up is a big one. We got to rustle to stay even or ahead of it.'

Cuyler waited only for a bite of supper, then saddled up again and hit the road for Sycamore. The night was well along and there was a big, ruddy moon in the sky before he got across the Brushies. He enjoyed the solitary ride. He had always liked the night under a benign sky. Space and quiet and the breath of the hills lifting all about him. Coyotes yammering on lonely ridge tops and the pure, cool call of the nighthawk drifting down from somewhere up among the powdered stars. It was, Cuyler decided, a kind of country that got hold of a man and held him.

It was well past midnight when he reached

Sycamore and the cavernous bulk of the covered bridge lifted before him. So he pulled off to one side along the river and slept the remaining hours of darkness out, not far from the wagon camp, his saddle for a pillow. In the crisp, dew-sweetened dawn he went over to the wagon camp.

Jess Petty was long and gaunt and silver-headed and his wife, a stout, jolly woman, invited Cuyler to breakfast with them. Cuyler put his proposition briefly.

'There are hay ranches, up along the Sarco River valley, and I need hay and lots of it, for my mules. I don't want to take any of my wagons off the wheat haul to go after it. I'd like to make a deal with you folks to hit these hay ranches, buy up and haul the fodder back here, where my wagons can pick it up on their return trips to Capell, when, for the most part, they travel empty. You won't run into any hostility here like you did up on the plains. How about it?'

'Suits me,' declared Jess Petty. 'Me and these other outfits need work. I know good hay when I see it. Nobody will euchre me on that point. Far as I'm concerned, it's a go.'

They settled other angles of the deal and then Cuyler rode on into Sycamore, where he spent much of the rest of the day, cleaning up a number of business items with the river boat freight offices. It was well into the afternoon when he started back for Capell.

The road ran arrow-straight across the flatness of Sarco Valley, but once into the foothills of the Brushies, began to wind and twist as it climbed slowly to the summit. Here it crossed through a shallow pass and, dropping down a short distance on the east side, turned sharply left to run in a long straightaway across the flank of a steep canyon side. Above and below the road the canyon was choken with scrub oak, manzanita and chemisal brush. The late afternoon air lay hot and still, sweetly pungent with the breath of leagues of space and earth and rocks and growing things.

Down in the canyon depths shadows lay, blue and smoky and restful and on the far side of the defile, where a series of little benches ran and where wild lilac and toyon berry thickets grew, Cuyler saw a pair of yearling deer already beginning to feed.

Again the feeling came to Cuyler that this was good country, with, for the most part, good people in it. Perhaps in time all difficulties would smooth out on the Vaca Plains, old enmities and grudges die and the ominous clash of interests be stilled. If these things came to be, then an era of prosperity lay ahead for all.

As always of late, when he was alone, Gene Cuyler's thoughts came around to Paula Juilliard and that thought now brought him to a grave consideration of Pierce Pomeroy, too. Sam Reeves had said that Pomeroy was mighty fond of Paula. How deeply, Cuyler wondered uneasily, was this sentiment reciprocated, if at all?

Pomeroy had been out to the J L to visit Paula and he had taken her to the dance. How stunning she had been in that blue evening dress! Cuyler's pulse quickened as he recalled it. Paula had told him she had hoped he'd be at the dance and that she would have danced with him if he had.

Pierce Pomeroy. How were you to figure Pomeroy, with his masked eyes and deep-locked thoughts? For a moment, mused Cuyler, there in the hotel lobby an open clash between the banker and himself had all but broken. There was that remark Pomeroy had made concerning the ownership of the freight outfits and a strange, disquieting statement it had been. True, Pomeroy held Cuyler's note, with a chattel mortgage on all of his wagons and mules, put up as collateral. And Pomeroy could always call that note and take over the outfits unless he was able to produce the cash to redeem it.

It wasn't, decided Cuyler, a pleasant possibility to have hanging over one's head. He got out the makings and rolled a smoke as he jogged along, his face gravely serious. The quicker, he thought, he could get the money together and clear that note up, the better for his future peace of mind. He also decided that it might not be wise to attempt to expand too fast.

Abruptly, into these troubled thoughts, carrying across the warm, still air came the faint clashing of yoke bells, coming from the north end of the straightaway, where the road looped steeply through several side gulches before swinging about a sharp point. Cuyler's moody eyes cleared. These were his wagons coming, rolling out the wheat. His wagons yet, and he'd keep them so, one way or another. He'd expected to meet them, somewhere along in the Brushies and now there they were, not far up ahead.

The song of the yoke bells grew louder as Cuyler approached within a hundred yards of the turn at the far end of the straightaway. That was when the shot sounded, from somewhere along the main ridge top, almost it seemed, directly above him. Thin and snarling and unmistakable. A rifle shot!

On the heels of the ripping, crackling echoes of the shot, the even beat of the advancing yoke bells broke cadence, became a mad, jangling, wild alarm. Then, out of the swift downpitch of a gulch end and into the sharp turn at the end of the straightaway, came wildly running mules, leaders, swing, pointers and wheelers. Behind came the wagon, towering, ponderous, driverless and charging madly.

Instinctively the pointers tried to do their job. They tried to jump the chain and steer the onrushing wagon safely through the turn. But

128

the chain, looping like a treacherous snake, cut the feet from under the near pointer, dropping the animal heavily beneath the desperately fighting hoofs of the rearing, lunging wheelers.

There was no chance now for the wagon. It was completely out of control, a massive, wild monster. It rumbled wide on the turn to the crumbling edge of the road where, for one dread second it seemed to be hanging in space. Then it toppled far, went over and was gone, the whipping pole lifting the wheelers like struggling insects and throwing them into oblivion, while the writhing clattering chain, slithering past the road edge, dragged pointers, swing and lead mules with it.

The leaders were the last to go, fighting and scrambling madly, eyes distended with terror, the bells on their hame yokes shrilling a dissonance of utter tragedy.

The wagon struck for the first time, blotting out all other sounds in a heavy, booming crash. Twice more the echoes rolled as the wagon struck again and again, tumbling. One final crash and the ominous echoes thinned and ran away into stillness. Faintly, and once only, did a dying whisper of silvery bells drift up from the canyon depths. After that, just utter silence, while dust came rolling and welling up past the road edge.

CHAPTER SEVEN

TANGLED TRAILS

Hack Dowd lay dead at the edge of the road, right there in the steepest part of the downpitch leading out of the gulch turn into the head of the straightaway. A tangled, crumpled figure, shot through the heart by a high-powered rifle bullet.

Gene Cuyler straightened up from examining the wrinkled, leathery old-timer and looked with bleak eyes at Bill Wragg and the other teamsters who had stopped their outfits and come hurrying up with ready rifles.

'I heard the shot,' said Cuyler stonily. 'It came from up on the ridge above. Whoever did it had it figured just right. They knew that Hack would be leaning into his brake strap, easing the wagon down this sharp pitch. They knew that when they dropped him and the brake went loose the wagon would roll out of control and go over the edge into the canyon at the turn. They figured it fine and made a dead center shot. Poor old Hack—he never knew what hit him.'

Bill Wragg cursed with helpless fury. Ott Wylie snarled. 'If we bust right up into that brush maybe we might get a crack at the rotten whelp, whoever he is.'

130

Cuyler shook his head. 'Not a chance, Ott. Whoever did it had it all figured and is on the move by this time, his getaway all figured and planned for. He may have left some sign and I'll have a look for it, later on. But there's nothing you boys can do now but keep on rolling. Put Hack up on your wagon, Bill, and take him on to Sycamore. Make all the necessary arrangements there and I'll foot the bill. Where's Mike Kenna? His wagon is generally rolling the lead.'

'One of his wheelers busted a trace just short of the hills and he pulled out to let the rest of us by while he made the repair,' explained Bill Wragg. 'He'll be along. Hack's outfit—do you think—?'

'I'll take a look at it,' Cuyler said. 'I know what I'll find and it won't be much. If there's anything to be salvaged I'll tell Kenna about it when he comes by. The rest of you get along.'

With Hack Dowd taking his last ride on one of his beloved freight wagons, the long column of mules and freighters rumbled through, and it seemed to Gene Cuyler that the merriness of the yoke bells had become a measured dirge, escorting a fallen warrior to his last rest. The final outfit past, Cuyler went down over the road edge to survey the wreckage.

The big Merivale wagon was over a hundred feet down the canyon, wedged upside down in a thicket of tough scrub oaks. It was a complete wreck. The wheels were smashed, spokes

131

splintered, hubs split, felloes shattered, heavy iron tires bent and twisted. The reach was broken, the pole snapped short off. The body of the wagon was kindling wood.

Fat sacks of wheat were scattered in a wild cascade above and below the ruined wagon. Some of the sacks had burst open, spilling their golden contents everywhere. Yet it wasn't so much the sight of the ruined wagon or the scattered wheat that put the bleak chill in Cuyler's eyes. It was the thought of Hack Dowd and of the mules. Poor, dumb, faithful mules—twelve of them...

It was a bitter, heartrending business, but it had to be done in the name of mercy. Three of the mules, both wheelers and one of the pointers were already dead. For the others there was no shred of hope. Broken legs, twisted joints, crushed ribs...

Climbing over rocks, around gnarled scrub oaks, through clumps of manzanita and chemisal and toyon brush, Cuyler went along the mad tangle of chain, harness and doomed animals. Nine times did the hoarse, thudding bark of his six-shooter echo. Then, taut and white about the lips, he climbed back to the road, punching out the empties of his second cylinder loading. He was building a smoke with shaking fingers when Mike Kenna came rolling his outfit through.

When Cuyler told of the tragedy, Mike let out a low, hoarse cry of anger.

'What dirty, black-hearted hound could have done a thing like that? And it would have been me who got it instead of poor old Hack, if that trace hadn't busted and held me up for a spell. Gene lad, the wagon—the mules—?'

'Wagon a complete loss and the mules all dead. On the return trip, Mike, you'll have the boys stop and salvage what they can. Chain and harness and other gear, along with what wheat they can where the sacks did not break open.'

Mike Kenna was sick and stunned. 'I'd ask only to get my bare hands on that dirty fiend,' he gritted thickly. 'Ah! The pity of it—'

'I'm going to see if I can pick up the killer's trail now,' said Cuyler wearily. 'See you in Capell tomorrow afternoon, Mike.'

It was a steep and difficult climb, up from the road to the top of the ridge. Cuyler made it on foot, leading his horse behind him. On the crest he mounted, which got him above the brush and enabled him to look around.

It was a wilderness, up there on that main ridge. Cuyler quickly saw that there were a dozen places where a man could have lain in wait to turn loose that fatal, treacherous shot. Underfoot the ground was hard and rocky and a man, particularly if he be on foot in that particular section, could move about at will, leaving no sign at all. There were several points of rock, jutting above the tangle of brush, where the killer could have waited and fired his fatal shot. Cuyler examined all of these, but found nothing.

He spent a full hour in fruitless search of any kind of evidence which might give him a lead to work on, but he found nothing at all. On all sides the brush spread, thick, masking and mocking. It was, he decided finally, like looking for the proverbial needle in a haystack and with no more chance of success. He went back down to the road and headed for Capell.

He got there just in time to put up his horse and get a bite of supper at the Elite Café before it closed up for the night. In there he found Steve Sears, joshing with a friendly biscuit shooter. At sight of Cuyler's face, Steve sobered instantly.

'Something wrong, boss. What is it?'

Cuyler told him and Steve's blackened eyes squinted in misery. 'That's dirty—that's rotten! Hack Dowd—the mules—and no sign at all of who did it, Gene?'

'Not a thread of sign. From now on, kid, we watch every angle. You bed down out around the corrals tonight. Keep your gun handy. You see or hear any prowlers, don't bother to ask questions. Start shootin'. This game is getting rough, and rough is the way we'll play it.'

After he'd eaten, Cuyler prowled the town from end to end, his jaw grim and his eyes bleak with frost, and with a definite chip on his shoulder. Deep within him burned a thin, cold, unquenchable rage which could only be eased

134

through violent conflict of some sort. He would have welcomed that conflict, fists, guns, sudden death—anything! Anything but this feeling of helpless, trapped impotency.

For he had no idea which way to turn to get a line on the killer of Hack Dowd. He could guess, but that meant nothing. And whether this was the opening move of a new attack by Joe Justin and Teede Hunnewell was definitely a guess, which logic could pretty well refute. For if the hostile cattle interests were responsible, why, for instance, should they have been content to drop just one of his teamsters and wreck only one outfit?

Loss of one man and one outfit, while it would hurt him and hurt him bad, would still not crush him completely, which was what it was logical to reason as the thing the cattle interests wanted to do. Yet, if it wasn't the cattle interests that were responsible for this thing, who else could it be? Who else could be gunning for his hide, and why?

Maybe Gatt Ivance, this gunman now riding for Joe Justin. Ivance, whom he had helped run out of the Burney country, where Ivance had been a killer on the wrong side of a timber war. That Ivance hated him ferally and had threatened vengeance, and that Ivance's hate would certainly be even more bitter and consuming since being gun whipped that night when the cattle crowd had tried to trap him in town, Cuyler was certain. It could have been

Ivance. Yet, would the gunman strike this way when what he really yearned to do was shoot the life out of him, not one of his men?

It was a bitter, bleak question that Cuyler carried back and forth with him as he prowled the town, and he came up with no more answer than he'd been able to find back there in the Brushies up on the ridge above the scene of the tragedy.

His antagonistic mood got Cuyler nowhere. Capell was as quiet as he'd ever seen it, with little evidence of people anywhere. So he went to the hotel finally, where he found Sam Reeves taking his usual nightly licking from Pierce Pomeroy in their chess game. Sam Reeves looked up, nodded, then held a steady scrutiny.

'Something is biting you, friend,' he said. 'What is it?'

Cuyler pulled up a chair and told the story curtly and bluntly. Sam Reeves whistled softly.

'That was a lousy trick! I could cheerfully pull on the rope that would swing the whelp who did it.'

'Here, too!' snapped Pierce Pomeroy, his black eyes going bleak. 'Good Lord! Who'd be low enough to do a thing like that? A good man gone, a wagon and string of mules gone. Sam, this takes all the edge off this game of ours. Let's forget it for tonight.'

Sam Reeves nodded, pushed his chair back. 'That shot cost you a chunk of money, Gene.'

Cuyler nodded slowly. 'Yeah, it did, plenty

of money. But I'm not thinking about that right now. I'm thinking of Hack Dowd and twelve poor, helpless mule critters. I saw them go over the grade, right in front of me. I don't know that I'll ever forget that picture. The leaders, they were the last to go. How they fought against the remorseless pull of that chain! And the look in their eyes—!'

Cuyler's voice went hoarse and thick and he scrubbed a hand across his face as though trying vainly to wipe away the haunting picture. He went on bitterly.

'Then I had to go down over the edge after them and use my six-shooter. One of these days I'll come up with the rat responsible for it all. When I do—!' He made a short, swift gesture, as though he were wiping out something venomous and forever unclean.

Pierce Pomeroy nodded. 'I know just how you feel. A thing like that puts the iron in a man's soul. Human nature is a strange thing. There have been countless evidences of man's nobility, yet just as many of a depravity that would shame the devil himself.'

'I dunno about that,' growled Sam Reeves. 'But I do know that the more I think of such rotten business, the madder I get. I think we could all stand a big drink, and I got the bottle.'

*   *   *

Next morning Cuyler's problem was still riding

him grimly and would not let him rest. So he saddled up and rode, heading nowhere in particular but just driven by a need for movement. Hours later he ended up in the low, folded hills to the east, where Ben Loftus had his drill rig set up and working.

A pair of ponies, hitched to the pole of the run-around, jogged their monotonous, never-ending circle. The bull wheel of the rig spun ponderously and the drill cable jerked up and down, clanking. Ben Loftus threw up a welcoming hand as Cuyler came riding in.

'Down thirty feet and into water already,' cried the cattleman triumphantly. 'Sort of a pumice formation and just shot full of water. I'm going down another fifty feet and then put a pump test on it. I'll be satisfied with five hundred gallons an hour, but I got a hunch it may run twice that much. Mister, this is a well!'

Cuyler said, 'You talk the lingo as though you'd been at this sort of business all your life.'

'Been reading up on it ever since you pounded the idea into my head,' admitted Loftus cheerfully. 'Say, you got a look about you, Cuyler. Anything wrong?'

Cuyler told him and Loftus cursed harshly, his face going dark with anger. 'That's as bad as anything I ever heard. Got any idea of who did it?'

'Not yet, but I expect to.'

'Hunnewell's orders—or Justin's, do you think? I haven't seen anything of them lately.'

Cuyler shrugged. 'No answer yet. It won't be pleasant when I find it.'

A buckboard came rolling up from the flats.

'Noon grub,' said Loftus. 'Paula said she'd bring it out. Rest your saddle and eat with us, Cuyler.'

It did not make a bit of difference, thought Gene Cuyler, whether this girl was in a gingham house dress, in riding togs, in a dance frock or, just as she was now, with plain skirt and blouse. She still took your breath away. As she pulled the buckboard to a halt, she gave him a bright, quick smile.

'Where's Candy?' asked Loftus. 'Thought she'd be out, too.'

Paula shrugged. 'She saddled up and rode off a couple of hours ago. I waited for her as long as I could, then came ahead before you men starved to death.'

Loftus frowned, but said no more about it.

They sat around a square of tarp spread on the ground, ate and talked well drilling and water and range and wheat farming.

'Time will come when there'll be wheat on every flat acre of the plains,' said Loftus. 'I've had that hunch for a long time but was just too pig-headed to admit it, even to myself. But now that I've come around to accepting the inevitable, damned if it ain't a big relief.'

'There's a lot of good graze in a wheat field after the crop has been harvested,' observed Cuyler. 'I've seen cattle take on fat, working through wheat stubble. I think you could probably find wheat men ready to talk business with you on that angle. If you run short of grass during the fall months, think it over.'

'You keep on, you'll have me and those wheat men friendly as chipmunks in a hollow log.' Loftus grinned.

'I could think of worse things. There never is any percentage either way in a range war. After all, folks got to learn to live together in this world.'

The meal finished, Loftus and his men got back to work. Cuyler helped Paula Juilliard pack up and stow the eating gear, then jogged along beside the buckboard as the girl drove off. After a couple of hundred yards of silence, Paula spoke abruptly.

'We've a great deal to thank you for Gene— Uncle Ben and I. And Candy, too.'

Startled, Cuyler looked at her.

'Why? As I see it, things should be the other way around. You've done more than you dream, bringing your uncle around to a better point of view. And that's only part of it. I owe you so much I never could pay it back.'

'I could never have brought Uncle Ben around without the aid of the way you handled several pretty shaky situations,' insisted Paula. 'The idea of violence, the way things were at first, had me frightened to death all the time. Once there was a cattle and sheep war on these plains. That war cost me my father, who was

Uncle Ben's partner. I've never forgotten.'

'So far, violence of some sort has ridden at my shoulder,' reminded Gene somberly. 'And it's still there.'

She looked at him. He was staring straight ahead, his face bleak with the shadow of his thoughts. He sat his saddle with all the unconscious ease a born cattle hand might have known. There was a hard, flat breadth to him about the shoulders, tapering down to leanness at the waist. His features were strong, ruggedly set. There was power and tenacity in the hard angle of his jaw. His hands were big and square and capable, his wrists muscular. He was, she thought, a man who would take a lot of whipping before he'd ever surrender. She was startled and disturbed at his abrupt and shadowed gravity, but she did not question it. She did not speak again until the ranch building came in view.

'You must be very careful who you trust, Gene. Who you accept at face value as a friend and confidant.'

It was Cuyler's turn to be startled. He looked at her keenly. 'Just who and what are you taking about?'

Paula shook her dark head. 'I can't say more because I'm not entirely sure. But once I am, I'll speak frankly.'

At the J L headquarters, she left the buckboard and its contents to the ranch cook and his helper and walked over to the ranchhouse with Cuyler beside her, leading his horse. Her head came just even with the peak of his shoulder. She climbed the porch steps a little way and stood looking down at him, that grave, faint smile touching her lips.

Then she turned and sped into the house.

Two miles back along the town trail, Cuyler met up with two riders. Candy Loftus and Blaze Doan.

Candy flushed at Cuyler's glance, then tossed her yellow head defiantly. Doan gave off a surly scowl. Cuyler swung his horse to block the trail, his frosty eyes boring at the cowpuncher. Doan still bore plenty of evidence of his fight with Steve Sears.

'Just a minute, Doan,' said Cuyler. 'Got a question I want to ask you. Where were you yesterday afternoon along about four o'clock?'

'Your business, you think?' blurted Doan.

'I'm making it so. I want to know. I want to get some of you junipers placed. You—and Huntoon, for instance. All right, I asked you a question and I want a straight answer.'

'I don't owe you a damn thing,' retorted Doan. 'Where I was and what I was doing is all my affair and none of yours. Get off the trail!'

He made as if to push past Cuyler, who drove his horse in hard, bringing him knee to knee with the rider. Cuyler's shoulders swayed forward and his tone carried the thin bite of a whiplash.

'You got one more chance, Doan—then I

knock an answer out of you if I have to. Let me explain. Yesterday afternoon, at about the time I mentioned, one of my teamsters was shot off his wagon, out along the Sycamore road. The wagon and mules went over the grade. Whoever pulled that dirty trick was laying out above the road in the brush. So now—where were you about that time?'

Cuyler heard Candy Loftus catch her breath. 'He wasn't there,' she cried. 'Blaze was out riding with me.'

'I hope you're right, Candy,' said Cuyler without turning his head. 'But we'll let Mister Doan answer for himself.'

Doan was obviously startled at what Cuyler had told him. Now he shrugged sulkily. 'She's right. I wasn't anywhere near the Brushies. Haven't been, in weeks.'

Cuyler saw that Doan was speaking the truth. He swung his horse away, looked at the girl.

'You got an argument coming up with your father. He was expecting you out where he's drilling that well. You'll run into that willow switch yet.'

Candy tossed her head again, but there was a pale, big-eyed look about her now. She spurred her pony into a run and Doan, scowling more deeply, hurried off after her.

It was hot, up there in the brush on top of the main ridge of the Brushy Hills. Gene Cuyler had been there since early morning. He had a

143

rifle and a pair of field glasses that he had borrowed from Gil Saltmarsh. He had found the highest eminence he could and had settled there in the gray chemisal and the ruddy-barked manzanita. All day long he had waited and watched and he had seen nothing except a few buzzards sailing high against the sky on effortless wings, some deer browsing, and once a scant glimpse of day-prowling coyote. But no sign of anything human, afoot or in the saddle.

He had heard his wagons coming, yoke bells singing in the distance, then passing below him, then faintly carrying back from the south and west as they topped the pass and rolled on down into Sarco Valley. Now, his vigil over, he sought his horse and rode back the long miles to Capell.

It was dusk when he got there. He turned his horse into the corrals, crossed to one of the watering troughs where water was splashing from a feed pipe. He drank deeply, took water in his cupped hands and scoured the sweat and dust from his face. He dampened his hair and the night wind felt cool and good, brushing his face.

As he climbed out of the corral he stiffened, dropped a hand to his gun. For there, indistinct in the gloom was a rider, a rider who had come up quietly while Gene was at the trough, the splash of water filling his ears against other sound.

'Who is it?' rapped Gene harshly. 'Looking

144

for someone?'

The answer came with some diffidence. 'You'll do.'

'Candy! Candy Loftus! What brings you here, youngster?'

'Is—is Steve Sears around?' she asked.

'Sorry. Steve is with the wagons, down at Sycamore. What did you want to see him about?'

Candy was silent for a moment and when she did speak her voice was subdued.

'I couldn't forget what you told Blaze Doan—about a driver of yours who was shot off his wagon. Then—then Dad was telling me more about it. It was pretty awful. I kept thinking how it might have been Steve, how at another time it might still be Steve. So I wanted him to know I was glad he danced with me the other night. And that I don't—don't hate him like I said.'

'That—from you!' exclaimed Gene, definitely astounded. 'If Steve had been here, would you have said that to his face?'

'Yes,' said Candy quietly. 'I would have.'

Gene moved up beside her horse. 'Shake, youngster. I'm apologizing for a lot of things I've said to you and for things I've thought. The right strain has been there all the time, only just covered up by thoughtlessness. Steve was right all the time when he vowed you were quite a girl. So I promise you this. As far as I possibly can, Candy, I'll keep Steve away from

145

any real trouble. Now we're friends, you and me?'

Her hand was small and warm in Gene's big paw. She nodded.

'Yes, we're friends.'

She swung her horse away, pulled up just a trifle. 'You take mighty good care of yourself, Gene. For somebody else.'

Then she was gone, flying through the early night.

For the next ten days Gene left the corrals and wagon yard only to sleep and eat. With Gil Saltmarsh's help he had rounded up half a dozen men about town and put them to work under the eye of Luke Malcolm and real progress was made in the repairs Gene had figured on. Along with enlarging corrals, building more feed sheds and repairing the old adobe, they rigged up a derrick with which to stack the baled hay that was beginning to come in on the wagons from Sarco Valley, where Jess Petty was doing a good job of buying.

There were other things to be done. The fate of Hack Dowd and his outfit weighed on the minds of everyone. There was no guarantee that the slinking killer of Hack Dowd might not strike again at any time and any place. Every teamster knew this and, while there was no slightest thought of shirking his part, each man showed the weight of strain. They were sober, intent, hard-eyed.

Each round trip to Sycamore, Gene Cuyler

laid up one wagon and team for a rest, revolving the procedure all down the line. He took Skeet Yore, who was the best rifle shot among all the skinners, off the wagons completely. Each morning, with rifle and field glasses, Skeet rode away into the Brushies, to watch the high ridges for skulkers. Each night he returned, to report all quiet and peaceful.

Wheat and more wheat moved out, and it was well that it did, for with the lumber and labor costs, and what it took to pay Jess Petty for hay and hauling, Cuyler's cash reserve was always at a minimum. He kept remembering that he had to hold out enough to meet the interest of his bank loan.

Memory of his clash with Pierce Pomeroy in the hotel lobby the evening of the dance, and of the remark Pomeroy had made concerning ownership of the freight outfits, always lay at the back of Gene's mind. But as the days went by with the banker more affable and friendly than he'd ever been, Cuyler's uneasiness over the affair began to leave him. After all, that night a lot of tempers had been scratched, his own included.

A number of times Pierce Pomeroy dropped around to survey the improvements taking place. And his attitude was always that of complete approval.

'You got the right idea, Cuyler,' he said. 'To do a job right a man has to have the right tools and the proper facilities. A haywire setup stays haywire, with no future. And it is a sign of sloppy thinking. I can see the time ahead when thirty to forty freight outfits will be rolling in and out of Capell at the peak of the wheat harvest. Right now Capell is more prosperous than I've ever seen it, which means good business for everyone.' He waved an encompassing hand. 'Don't worry about the interest payments on that note. I can see you're spending a lot of ready cash here. If you need more, just let me know. And if you see a chance to grab up some more freight rigs, do it—and I'll foot the bill.'

Pomeroy swung his glance around, nodding with satisfaction. 'This I like to see,' he went on. 'Planning, constructive progress. You've done a great job, Cuyler.'

'Any luck so far in picking the property up at that tax sale you mentioned?' asked Gene.

'Going through the works right now,' nodded the banker. 'Nothing to worry about there. I'll handle it.' He smiled briefly. 'You'll never know how close I came to turning you down that first night you hit me for a loan, man. Here you were, a complete stranger, a man I'd never laid eyes on before. At the moment, the way things were going, a loan on a wagon freighting proposition was about the poorest risk a man could think of. I talked regular banking procedure to you, when any banker in his right mind would have turned you down flat. But you had a look about you

148

and the whole idea was so daring it appealed to me because of the sheer risk of it. So don't let anyone tell you, my friend, that a banker hasn't sporting blood in him.'

Gene grinned. 'I was lucky that I bumped into one who had. And you're right about the future of this business. It's all here. But I wish,' and here the grin faded, 'I knew what was in the minds of Joe Justin and Teede Hunnewell. They're far too quiet.'

Pomeroy shrugged. 'One thing we know. We're digging in stronger all the time. They'll find us plenty hard to handle as time goes by. No lead I suppose, so far, on that damned dry-gulcher?'

Gene shook his head. 'Not a smidgin. But I got a man out guarding, all the time.'

That night Gene drew Steve Sears aside. 'Lady friend of yours dropped around the other evening, kid.'

'Lady friend!' blurted Steve, surprised. 'What lady friend?'

'Didn't know you had more than one,' grinned Gene. 'Candy Loftus.'

'Candy! To see me?'

'That's right. I told her you were down at Sycamore.'

Steve groaned. 'I would have to be away. What did she want?'

'Why, she wanted you to know that she was glad you danced with her and that she didn't mean a lot of mad things she said about you.

Now keep your shirt on. This doesn't mean you're to high-tail right out to the J L and take the little lady in your arms. But it's a thought to keep you happy and a promise that the next time you meet up with her, Candy won't throw rocks at you.'

'Doggone!' glowed Steve boyishly. 'Oh— doggone! She's wonderful, that girl is.'

The fact that no further trouble had developed along the road across the Brushies and that night after night Skeet Yore reported in that all was quiet and peaceful along the high ridges, did not cause Gene Cuyler to drop his purpose of paying off for Hack Dowd and the lost outfit. Yet it was a puzzling state of affairs.

Just that one isolated attack with no follow-through did not make sense. Gene was beginning to wonder if, after all, the whole thing wasn't the product of some private affair of Hack Dowd's. Maybe someone had had a grudge against old Hack, some ancient cause for hatred which had made them lay out in the brush to get him, with what might happen to his wagon and mules of no concern to them. But that was merely a guess, too. There was, Gene concluded, nothing to do but keep on guarding and waiting. If no further hostile act showed, fine and dandy. But he could not take the chance of being caught off guard again.

A couple of nights later, Gene was up at the store, talking business with Gil Saltmarsh, when Skeet Yore came quietly in.

150

'Another blank today, Skeet?' asked Cuyler.

Skeet nodded and drew Gene over to the door.

'Somebody to see you, down at the corrals. A lady.'

'Lady? Candy Loftus?'

'No. Miss Juilliard.'

Cuyler hurried out and down the darkening street. Paula stood by her horse's head, a slim, tense figure in the palely stealing light of the first stars.

'Paula! Something wrong?'

'I believe so, Gene,' she answered slowly. 'At least it is something I feel you should know.' Her voice was low, taut and troubled. 'You remember what I said out at the ranch the other day, about you being careful who you accepted as friend and advisor at their face value? Well, you wanted to know who and what I meant, but I told you I wasn't sure then. Once I was, however, I'd tell you more.'

'I remember,' nodded Cuyler. 'And now— you're sure?'

'Yes. Gene, don't trust Pierce Pomeroy. Don't trust him an inch.'

'Pierce Pomeroy! Why—Paula—!'

'I know,' she said. 'Sounds crazy, doesn't it, with him virtually a partner of yours? For he is backing you, isn't he? With money, I mean? That night in the hotel, after the dance, when you and he had that little argument, I judged from his remarks that he had loaned you

151

money. That's right, isn't it?'

'That's right. He loaned me the money to buy up five wagon outfits. I had to put them and the rest of my outfits up as collateral. Yet I was lucky to negotiate the loan, else I'd never have been able to move the wheat I'm moving now. Sure, we've differed on a couple of points, but there's no real quarrel between us. We get along. Why shouldn't I trust him?'

'Because he hates you,' declared the girl. 'I saw that clearly in his eyes today. It is one of the few things I've ever been able to read in those black, veiled eyes of his. He even managed to cover that up quickly, but not before I'd seen and understood.'

Gene was honestly bewildered. He had figured from the first that Pierce Pomeroy was shrewd, plenty! And that in money matters he might be pretty cold and ruthless. Yet he could think of no reason why the banker should hate him. You didn't, he reasoned, hate a man yet loan him money. Gene said as much.

'Pierce Pomeroy,' said Paula, a low note of bitterness in her tone, 'never made a loan yet on the basis of whether he liked or disliked a man. Profit alone would be the only consideration there. This isn't easy for me to say, Gene, because it makes me seem pretty brazen. But it must be told if you are to fully understand. The reason Pierce Pomeroy hates you, is because he is jealous of you.'

Cuyler stood very still for a moment.

152

'Jealous—of me?'

He saw her dark head nod. 'Of you. Pierce Pomeroy was out to the ranch today. He asked me to marry him. It was the third time he had asked me. Before, I always managed to dodge the issue. Today he was insistent, even rough. I grew angry, told him what I really thought of him. That I detested him, that I'd always detested him. That was when he let the curtain in his eyes drop and for the first time since I've known him I was able to read some of his thoughts. And they weren't good thoughts, Gene.'

Cuyler reached for his smoking, began building a cigarette while he got his reasoning straightened out.

'But he's visited you, Paula, and you went to that dance with him. If you detested him, why did you accept his company?'

'Because,' she answered simply, 'Uncle Ben and I owe him money. Uncle Ben and I are equal partners in the J L ranch, you know. Father, who was Uncle Ben's partner, left his share to me. I've always felt that Pomeroy was holding that debt over my head like an invisible club. Today, in his anger, he admitted as much and swore he'd call the loan immediately. If he does, that will hurt Uncle Ben's and my plans for the future, a lot. But when I told Uncle Ben about it he was wildly furious. Not at me, of course, but at Pomeroy. He said if Pomeroy ever set foot on our range again he'd shoot him

153

on sight. But that isn't what I came to see you about. It's you, and your affairs with Pomeroy. Watch him, Gene—don't trust him at all!'

'And why should he be jealous of me?'

She was silent for a moment. 'That terrible night,' she said slowly, 'when Hunnewell and Justin and Gatt Ivance were out to hunt you down and kill you, when we stood in the gloom close to the front of the Hotel, Pierce Pomeroy was just inside the open window behind us. He—he accused me of willingly standing there, in your arms. He heard what we said. He said he could see us outlined against a light on the far side of the street and so saw you—kiss my hair. You did, you know. And that was when he began hating you. All this he told me today, swept away by his anger. He even started to voice a threat against you, Gene—but managed to catch himself in time. Now you know.'

She turned, swung into her saddle, reining away a trifle. In another moment she would be gone.

'Has he real cause to be jealous of me, Paula?' asked Cuyler softly.

'There was never a time when I did not detest Pierce Pomeroy. But—I rode here tonight to tell you, didn't I?'

With this enigmatic answer, Paula Juilliard shook her reins and moved away into the dark.

CHAPTER EIGHT

CRIMSON TERROR

Gene Cuyler stood right where he was, smoking his cigarette down to the last ash. Growing excitement was rippling all through him, for his mind was vitalized to a brand-new line of thought on a number of things. When he finally went back up town his quick, alert stride told of his quickening thought. But he had everything well masked when he sauntered into the hotel.

Pierce Pomeroy and Sam Reeves were playing chess. There was a soiled, much thumbed newspaper lying on a near-by chair and Cuyler seated himself and apparently buried himself in reading. But this was pretense only, as he covertly studied the banker. And Cuyler wondered if it was imagination, stimulated by what Paula Juilliard had told him, which made him for the first time read into Pomeroy's absorption in the game a hard, poised, wolfish intentness, the tense crouch, waiting for the leap and the kill.

And perhaps it wasn't imagination, for abruptly Pomeroy made a move and rapped out, 'Checkmate!'

'Doggone you, Pierce,' wailed Sam Reeves. 'You don't waste a lick of time in knockin' a man's brains out, once you get the chance.'

'I play to win,' said the banker curtly. 'If you do not play to win, it's no contest and no interest.'

'Set 'em up again,' said Reeves. 'I'll try and make you sweat, this time.'

A half hour drifted by. Cuyler stirred, yawned and put the paper down. Pomeroy half turned in his chair.

'Got any line at all on that dry-gulcher yet, Cuyler?'

'Yes, and no,' answered Cuyler easily. 'Nothing definite, but at least not up against a blank wall, like before.'

'What do you mean? That you've struck a trail of some sort?'

'Call it a trail of thinking,' said Cuyler. 'Before, all I could do was figure that it must have been the cattle interests who had that killing pulled. Working from that angle I didn't get anywhere. Then, of a sudden, I finally realized that there might be somebody else who had it in for me. Being an average sort of guy, I've made my enemies as well as friends as I go along. Hunnewell and Justin and Gatt Ivance ain't the only enemies. The minute I came to that conclusion I realized there were a lot of new angles I could approach this thing from. And so far I've found some of those angles plenty interesting.'

'Such as—?'

Cuyler shrugged, grinning. 'In my way I'm a

cautious sort. And I try and be fair. I don't like to have snap judgment thrown my way, so I try not to throw it at the other fellow. Once I strike a trail where the sign is really definite, I'll talk it over with you, Pomeroy. Well, me for the blankets.'

He stood up, stretched and yawned again and started to leave the room. He stopped as Sam Reeves gave a yelp of delight.

'Check—mate! Ha! That makes us even, Pierce. Man, you sure left yourself wide open that time, and I got you nailed to the mast!'

Cuyler watched Pomeroy. The banker was staring at the chessboard, a dark, angry flush on his face. He stood up and spoke thinly.

'That's right. I walked right into that one, Reeves. That's enough for tonight.'

Pomeroy left the hotel without another word. Cuyler looked at Sam Reeves.

'Doesn't lose very well, does he?'

'You know,' said the hotelkeeper soberly, 'I've been playing chess with Pierce for a long time. I've seen him make wrong moves before, but never as careless as this one which let me smear him. He acted like all of a sudden his mind had wandered off completely somewhere else. Wonder what could have bit him, all so quick?'

Cuyler shrugged again, saying nothing. But as he spun a smoke into shape, a cool, speculative gleam was in his eye. He moved out on to the porch, sidled along to the darkest

157

end, tossed his cigarette aside without lighting it, dropped off the end of the porch and let keening eyes and ears sweep the street.

He saw Pierce Pomeroy's precisely striding figure blend and disappear into the blackness of an alley mouth on the far side of the street. Cuyler crossed over, listening, heard steps dying out at the far end of the alley. He followed on through.

Beyond were the sprawled outskirts of the town. A dim light shone murkily from the window of one shack. Cuyler saw a shadowed figure drift past this window, merge and vanish into the dark bulk of the cabin.

Cuyler circled, came up on the dark side of the cabin, then edged around a corner and up to the window. A lamp with a badly sooted chimney stood on a table and there was a bunk against the far wall of the place. Standing before the table, jabbing stiffened fingers for emphasis while he talked, was Pierce Pomeroy, the murky lamp laying a light cast across his features which gave him an almost Machiavellian look. Half sitting, half lounging on the untidy bunk, whiskey glass in hand, was Hitch Gower!

Gene Cuyler could not make out what was being said between the two, but he did not care. For now his thoughts were snapping and crackling like a string of firecrackers.

There had been far more truth than he realized in what he had told Pierce Pomeroy, back there in the hotel. A new trail of thinking was what he'd said he'd found. The locked conviction he'd had before that the hostile cattle interests were in some way responsible for Hack Dowd's death and loss of a freight outfit, had blinded him to all other possibilities.

Now—why now it was as if a dam had broken and the waters held behind it running free and wild. So with his thoughts.

Heated argument was going on between the two men in the cabin. Once, the way Pomeroy moved around to stand over Hitch Gower, made it seem that the banker was going to manhandle the ex-muleskinner. But there was a six-shooter lying on the bunk beside Gower and the fellow dropped a hand to it. In the end, Pomeroy pulled a thick roll of bills from a pocket and slammed it down on the table. Then he turned abruptly and left the cabin.

Cuyler flattened against the cabin side, where the gloom lay thick. He stayed that way until Pierce Pomeroy's shadowy figure disappeared in the alley again on his way back to the hotel. Then Cuyler edged up to the window for another look.

Hitch Gower was counting the money Pomeroy had thrown on the table, licking a dirty thumb as he turned the bills over, one by one. He pocketed the money, drained his whiskey bottle, tossed it into a corner then set about getting gear together. Presently Gower blew out the lamp, left the cabin.

Cuyler followed him, soft-footed, and intent. Gower headed away from town, came to a little, ramshackle corral, from which he led a horse and began saddling it. Half drunk, Gower was careless. Cuyler got within two strides of him before the horse, tossing a restless head, gave warning.

Gower whirled heavily, grabbing for his gun. Gene Cuyler went in on him, fast! He caught Gower's wrist, forcing his hand away from the gun. He whirled his man, tripping him and as Gower went down, Cuyler fell across him. He drove a left forearm hard across Gower's throat, cutting off the yell he figured was probably forming there and drove his full weight on bunched knees into Gower's gross body.

Gower gasped and weakened. Cuyler pressed his strangling forearm deeper into Gower's throat and the fellow gave up trying for his gun, grabbing at Cuyler's arm with both hands, trying to shove it off his tortured throat. Cuyler brought his clenched right fist over and down in two short, smashing blows. The first found Gower's temple, the second the angle of his jaw. Gower went limp.

Half an hour later, Gene Cuyler was riding down the starlit road toward the wheat country. At lead behind him was Hitch Gower's horse and Gower was tied face down across the saddle of this one. He was groaning

160

and making choked sounds, but these sounds could not carry more than a few yards, for Gower was gagged with his own dirty handkerchief.

At the big main gate of Jim Nickerson's ranch, Cuyler reined in, lifting a quiet call.

'Hello—the guard!'

'Right here—and watching you!' came the harsh reply. 'Who are you and what do you want?'

'Gene Cuyler. And I got business with Jim Nickerson.'

Chain rattled as the guard appeared mysteriously from the night and began unlocking the gate. As Cuyler rode through the guard exclaimed, 'Wait a minute, Cuyler! Who's that you're luggin' on that horse?'

'The answer, I hope, to a pretty important question. You'd be doing me a big favor, friend, if you'd give me your word not to mention this to a single soul. Don't get excited. This hombre ain't dead. Not, maybe, that he doesn't deserve to be. But he's much more valuable alive, right now. When and if his time does come, the law will take care of that. But most important of all just now is that nobody outside of you and me and Jim Nickerson knows where he is.'

'Well,' admitted the guard, 'I can't see anything greatly wrong with an arrangement like that. Get along. I haven't seen a damn thing.'

Cuyler left both horses out in the shadow of the farm buildings then went over to the farm house where he had to rouse Nickerson from his bed. The wheat rancher listened to Cuyler's brief explanation, then began crawling into his clothes.

'I got just the place,' said Nickerson. 'A special storeroom I had built to keep the first seed wheat I brought in. I'd sent clear to Kansas for that wheat and paid a whopping price for it. So, while holding it for the planting, I put it in this storeroom where there wasn't a chance for a mouse or a rat to get at it. If the place was tight enough to keep a four-legged rat out, it ought to keep a two-legged one in. Let's go!'

Nickerson lighted a lantern and led the way to the storeroom, Gene Cuyler coming along behind, pushing a sick and groggy Hitch Gower ahead of him. Nickerson tossed a roll of old blankets on the floor, brought a bucket of clean water. Between them, he and Cuyler went through Gower's pockets carefully, making sure the fellow had no matches on him. Then they locked him in.

'I'll see he's fed regular, Gene,' said Nickerson. 'And nobody will know he's there but you and me.'

'Who's guarding your main gate tonight?' asked Cuyler.

'Sam Preston. Why?'

'He was a little curious when I came in,'

162

Cuyler explained. 'Which was natural, of course. He agreed not to let the word get out, but maybe if you spoke to him about it again, he'll be extra cautious.'

Nickerson nodded. 'I'll speak to Sam first thing tomorrow.'

'Who,' asked Cuyler, 'represents the law in these parts?'

The wheat rancher shrugged. 'There's a sheriff in Sycamore. But he don't get up this way very often. Which suits me all right, because he's an ex-cattleman and that puts his sympathies you know where.'

'Afraid of that,' said Cuyler. 'Which is why I'm sending off a letter to Deputy U.S. Marshal Cade Booker. Cade's a fine man and a good friend of mine. And while his authority doesn't really touch things like this, he represents something that'll put the fear of the Lord into Hitch Gower. Which is what we need to make Gower talk. I knew Cade when the Government sent him up to Burney to straighten up some lumber interests there and put a stop to certain private outfits who were cutting timber in Government forests where they had no right to be. I'll explain the whole thing to Cade and I know he'll show up, just as a personal favor. We'll hold Gower here until Cade arrives.'

'Whatever you say,' Nickerson agreed. 'Gower will keep.'

Cuyler rode back to Capell through the pale,

cold light of after-midnight stars. He put his weary horse up and then, in his room, did some letter writing before turning in.

When he came out of the Elite Café after breakfast the next morning, a buckboard and a heavy farm wagon were pulled up in front of Gil Saltmarsh's store. The buckboard looked familiar, so Gene went over there. A couple of farm hands, lugging a spool of barbed wire between them, came out to the wagon, skidded their burden into the vehicle, went back for more. Cuyler followed them in and knew the old, swift warming lilt to his pulse when he saw Paula Juilliard standing by the far end of the counter.

Her grave, small smile was waiting for him as he came up to her, hat in hand. But also in her eyes was a shadow of nervousness.

'Something is wrong, Paula?' he asked gently.

She shrugged. 'Uncle Ben is finding out what his past friendship with Teede Hunnewell and Joe Justin amounts to. For they've driven a lot of cattle into the hills around where Uncle Ben had just finished drilling his first well, got the mill up and the watering troughs full.'

'They would,' said Cuyler drily. 'Don't miss a trick, do they?'

'Uncle Ben is furious. He told them he hadn't gone to all the expense of drilling the well and putting the mill up just to water Looped H and Broken Bow cattle. They just

164

laughed at him and said that now there was good water as well as good grass in the eastern hills, they intended to get their share of it. There isn't a thing Uncle Ben can do about it, either. He can't keep a man at the troughs day and night to see that only J L cattle drink there.'

'So Teede Hunnewell is up and around again, eh?' murmured Gene. 'Glad to know that little thing. It could mean lots of things will start to break.'

'He can't walk very well yet,' said Paula. 'But he can ride. Those things that could start to break, they could be against you, too, couldn't they? Oh, Gene— there're so many things to be afraid of and about!'

He smiled at her. 'Drive that worry from your lovely eyes, girl. Everything will work out all right.' He went on, very softly, 'So often we meet in some public place where I can't say the things I'd like to say to you. And at other times you won't wait and give me a chance. Always you flit away from me, like a shaft of sunlight that touches me, warms me, then is gone. But there'll come a day, I promise you that, when you can't flit away from me, when you'll have to stand and listen to me.'

For a long moment they just stood there, looking at each other while that slow, tender smile lay warm on the girl's lips. For this brief moment they were worlds away from all the ordinary things of life.

Gil Saltmarsh's voice broke in on the magic moment.

'Hey, Gene—you got any idea what this is?'

Gil came over, followed by the two farm hands. Gil held out his hand. In it was a small lump of something, wrapped in heavy, damp paper.

'Smells like matches,' he said.

Cuyler took a look, his eyes narrowing.

'Where'd you get this?' he rapped.

One of the farm hands answered.

'Sam Preston give it to Huff and me when we drove out the main gate of the ranch on our way to town after this barbed wire Nickerson sent us for.'

'Where did Preston get it?'

'Damn—er, excuse me, miss. Darndest thing you ever heard of. Sam Preston stood main-gate guard last night. About an hour before dawn Sam hears a rider comin' along the road. Sam scrooges down low to get a line on this rider against the light of the stars. Sam figured the guy was either drunk or crazy, for as he rode along he was like he was chucking rocks. Sam said every so often this rider would stand in his stirrups and throw somethin'. One of the things he was throwin' lit in the edge of the wheat just back of where Sam was hid out. Sam heard it hit and soon as it got light he started lookin' around. This is what he found. It didn't make sense to him and when Huff and me come along he asked us. We didn't know

166

either, so Sam suggested we bring it to town and maybe Gil here might know. Mebbe it's somethin' that'll poison the wheat, huh?'

Gene Cuyler's voice went harsh and strained.

'It's worse than poison. It's fire! This is phosphorus. While it is kept wet this way it's inert. But once the sun gets on it and dries it out sufficiently, it begins to flame. I saw it used in that timber fight up around Burney. Gatt Ivance had a hand in that dirty business. Now he's brought the idea down here. Lord help the wheat farmers! Their fields of ripe, standing wheat will be in flames before this day is over. Maybe even now—!'

Paula Juilliard gave a cry of dismay, ran to the store door, stared off in the direction of Jim Nickerson's ranch. She turned and called.

'No sign of smoke yet, Gene. Quick! We'll take my buckboard. Maybe we can warn Nickerson and the others in time to do something. Quick!'

Cuyler handed the phosphorus chunk back to Gil Saltmarsh.

'Throw that out in the street and watch it, Gil. You'll soon see what I mean, now that the sun is climbing high. But get it out of your store before it burns the place down.'

Paula was up and had the reins as Gene untied the buckboard team. She kicked off the brake and had the rig in a skidding, scrambling turn as Gene hit the seat beside her. She laid on

167

the whip and the team stretched out into a wild gallop as they raced out of town.

*   *   *

They tore along through the morning sunlight, staring ahead with straining eyes, dreading what they might see at any moment. The first gust of flame, the first lifting coil of smoke. But as the racing ponies ate up the miles to Jim Nickerson's main gate, the threat had not materialized. The gate guard recognized Cuyler and let them through.

'What's all the rush about? What's—?'

Paula swung her whip and left the guard openmouthed and perplexed as the jouncing buckboard tore on toward the ranch buildings, where Nickerson and several farm hands were busy about a big McCormick harvester, making ready for the work ahead. Nickerson stepped out to meet the buckboard, wiping his hands on a greasy rag.

'Now what's wrong?' he boomed.

Cuyler told him, bluntly.

'You've not a second of time to waste, Jim. Get mowing machines out to cut fire lanes through the wheat. Get water barrels, wet sacks, hose, shovels and every man you have except someone to carry the warning to Pettibone and the rest. No time to argue or explain further, Jim. I know what I'm talking about. I know how phosphorus works. And

168

the sun is getting hotter by the minute. Move, *man*—move!'

Jim Nickerson read correctly the desperate urgency in Gene Cuyler's voice, in the strained intensity about his eyes. The big rancher whirled and began roaring orders. Men raced for the corrals. Horses were caught up and harnessed with furious speed. Two teams were hooked up to mowing machines and Nickerson yelled at the drivers.

'Cut a double swathe the whole length of the fields, parallel with the road and about a hundred yards in from the edge. Fast!'

The mowing machines, on cleated iron wheels, clanked and rattled away. Other men harnessed horses to a farm wagon. Barrels were loaded on, filled with water. Armfuls of empty grain sacks were piled in, shovels and hoes and pitchforks brought. Gene helped Paula up and climbed in himself. The wagon rumbled away, the driver urging the team to a run.

Then it was that Paula, hanging on desperately, cried, pointed.

'Look! Smoke!'

Sure enough, smoke it was, out at the edge of the wheat next to the road, some quarter of a mile north of the main gate. There the dread haze was lifting, pale gray at first, then darkening swiftly, above the first bright, licking tongue of flame.

Jim Nickerson groaned.

169

'There it goes! This can turn into complete hell!'

Within the space of minutes, Jim Nickerson's prophecy was perilously close to fact. Along the entire edge of the big field, facing the road, flame sprang up in half a dozen places and began eating into the precious wheat. Smoke billowed in sooty banners, rolling up to to stain a spotless sky. The flames spread, roaring and wicked.

A guard, seeing the first flame whirl up, started for it, but had not gone ten yards before another spike of fire leaped up almost beside him. He ran to this, tried to stamp it out, heard a crackling behind him, turned and saw more flame there. He backed away, stunned and bewildered, a gust of panic sweeping over him, because he did not understand.

Paula Juilliard stood in the racing farm wagon, wet to the waist by the water swilkering from the open-topped barrels. She clung to a barrel with one hand and to Gene Cuyler with the other. The wagon turned into the double swathe cut by the mowing machines which were out ahead, blades whirring urgently, already nearly hidden by the drifting smoke. At Nickerson's shouted orders men began dropping off the wagon, bundles of water-soaked sacks in their hands.

'Backfire!' yelled Nickerson. 'Backfire, then beat it out in the short stubble!'

Men ran along the east side of the cut

swathes, scratching matches, touching off fresh gusts of flame. They raked back the cut grain in the swathes, and any flame that tried to creep treacherously across the short stubble to get at the standing grain behind them, they beat out with wet sacks. They forced the line of fire they had started to burn to the east and so meet the roaring inferno coming from that side.

Gene Cuyler joined these men, with Paula Juilliard close beside him, lugging wet sacks. Gene lit the backfires and together they fought the flame away from the short stubble.

The smoke thickened to a bitter, sooty, choking pall and the heat took on a savage force and impact. No precious breath was wasted in words. Only in the distance was Jim Nickerson's big voice roaring, directing the fight. But soon even this was smothered and lost under the crescendo of hissing, crackling flame.

Sweat streamed down Gene Cuyler's face, broke out across his chest and back, turning his shirt black and wet. Smoke choked his lungs, lay in them like some intolerable weight. This same physical distress, he knew, was Paula's portion, and the knowledge hurt him.

Her glorious, shining hair had loosened and now fell about her face and shoulders, but she paid it no attention as she flailed valiantly away with her wet sack. A cinder, alive and wicked, whirled out of the smoke, struck her hair and clung. Cuyler saw, slapped it out, went on with the battle.

Full well he knew the danger that loomed all about them. Should the treacherous flames sneak across that cut stubble in any place and get behind them, they could very well be trapped and roasted to a crisp. This was more than merely fighting fire. This had become almost a fight for life.

The fire was an enemy, hungry, savage and relentless. Cuyler found himself cursing it as he fought it.

Once, in all that choking, sooty pall of smoke he lost sight of Paula where, a moment before, she had been right at his side. Quick fear twisted his heart and he ran back, calling hoarsely.

He found her, where she had gone back to beat out a creeping line of flame that had crawled almost halfway across the short stubble. In his relief he pulled her close to him.

'You must be careful, Paula,' he mumbled thickly.

There was a dry sob in her throat.

They lost all count of time and distance and the measure of human capacity and endurance. They became automatons, their moves mechanical. The heat was ghastly. Gene Cuyler crouched as low as he could and still keep his feet. Even so it seemed he could feel his skin crisping and shriveling. What air he did manage to drag into his strangled, tortured lungs seemed to do him no good, for it was as if the fire had sucked all the oxygen out of it.

There was more live flame just ahead and also a huge figure in the smoke, swinging a sack savagely. It was Jim Nickerson and the rancher was snarling and mumbling as he fought, as though at something alive.

They stumbled into each other, he and Nickerson, and the rancher croaked hoarsely at him.

'Go back the way you came, while I go north. Think we've got it—got it corraled, licked—! But make sure of every inch!'

Cuyler put an arm about Paula, half carrying her as they started back. She was near collapse, her strength gone. She had fought this thing to her limit, and past that limit. Cuyler wondered numbly that he was able to keep going, himself. He seemed dead from the waist down, half fried from there up. He tried to lick his lips and it was like sandpaper meeting sandpaper.

Gradually they moved into an area where the heat seemed slightly less. Here the backfire had burned well to the east, already beginning to meet the flames advancing from that side. And when they met, the flames towered high, like malignant demons struggling in death throes, voicing a thwarted fury in one final wild, seething roar. Then they dwindled and fell and left only the staining smoke and black ash.

173

Cuyler tightened his arm about Paula, supporting and guiding her. For the reaction had her fully now and she was faltering and sobbing convulsively. They met a scorched and blackened farm hand who gave them a canteen of water. They stumbled out into the safety of the side road and here Paula sank down, whimpering like a child. Cuyler made her drink from the canteen, then gulped a mouthful himself.

He knelt beside Paula, untied her neckerchief, soaked it with water, put a finger under her chin, tipped her face up and gently wiped away the worst of the soot and grime and tears.

'Steady, partner,' he comforted. 'Steady! Smile at me, just a little smile will do—while I wash your dirty little face. It's over and we've whipped it.'

Jim Nickerson came along, making a personal inspection of every foot of the blackened fire line. He was blistered and scorched, black with smoke and soot from head to toe. This ferocious thing had carved deep lines about his mouth, hollowed his eyes. He looked at Paula.

'The girl—she's all right? Not hurt or burned?'

'She's all right,' nodded Cuyler. 'Just a mite tuckered out, that's all.'

'A grand girl,' rumbled the rancher. 'Between the two of you, Gene—bringing me

174

the warning that enabled us to get going just in time, and then helping to fight the flames back—well, the two of you have just about saved my skin.'

Cuyler waved an arm toward the south.

'Pettibone and the others, Jim—not so lucky.'

Nickerson stared at the rolling clouds of smoke lifting from the fields down there.

'Tough,' he nodded. 'Mighty tough. Nothing we could do to help them now. This is what Hunnewell and Justin had up their sleeves all the time. This is why they've been laying quiet for so long. Waiting for the wheat to ripen and dry, so it would burn good.' His big voice thinned with a chilled anger. 'The dirty whelps! They want to make it this kind of a fight, do they? All right, this is the way it will be, from now on. I'll carry the fight to them. I'll shoot their cattle, I'll shoot their men, I'll shoot them—on sight! If they try and ride this road by day or night, they'll never leave it alive. Yeah, if this is the way they want it, this is the way they'll get it!'

A buckboard came racing along the main road, stopped at the gate. A long shout lifted. Cuyler stared through the thinning smoke.

'Gil Saltmarsh!' he exclaimed. 'He's got something on his mind. Let him in, Jim!'

Paula had quieted now and Cuyler helped her to her feet as Gil Saltmarsh brought his buckboard to a skidding halt beside them. His face was grim.

'Let's have it, Gil,' rapped Cuyler. 'Even if it's bad.'

'It's bad,' said Saltmarsh. 'This ain't the only place things are burning. Back at town your stacked hay and corrals are going up, Gene. Sam Reeves and other men about town are doing the best they can, but when I left to try and locate you, it didn't look as if anything much could be saved!'

CHAPTER NINE

CATTLE FOR WHEAT

The pile of baled hay which Gene Cuyler had been stacking up against the needs of his mules was one huge, ferocious, live cinder, giving off a blasting heat which made it impossible to approach. Because of the compactness of the bales it burned slowly, but it burned all over, in a thin, uprunning waterfall of flames.

There was nothing to be done about it. It would have taken powerful, drenching deluges of water to put it out and such means were unavailable in this lonely town of Capell. It was burning from the outside in, and it would burn for days.

Cuyler stared at it for a long time with bleak eyes, then turned his back on it, writing it off as

176

a complete loss. He surveyed the rest of the damage. Sections of the corrals were gone, along with most of the feed sheds. The windmill was intact, however, and was turning, pumping its streams of water into the troughs, which had been scooped dry by the hastily organized bucket brigade under Sam Reeves.

Paula Juilliard, blinking through her tears, cried softly.

'Gene—what have they done to you—?'

Cuyler looked at her. Despite the disarray of her hair, despite the grime and soot which smudged her face and hands and clothes, she stood the fairest sight his eyes had ever rested on. Beneath the soot on one soft cheek lay the sullen flush of fire scorch. Cuyler touched the spot very gently.

'That must be cared for right away. You've been wonderful. There are things in my heart I can't find words to speak. Now you must get along home, to rest and take care of yourself.'

She saw many things in his eyes, saw the caress in them that was for her, saw the hard, bitter chill of purpose that was for others. It frightened and thrilled her, all at the same time. She matched his courage with her own, speaking simply.

'I'll be waiting for you, Gene.'

She turned and walked away to her buckboard, passing within a stride of a gray-faced Pierce Pomeroy who had stood there watching all that passed between her and Gene

177

Cuyler. She passed Pierce Pomeroy and never saw him. For her eyes were fixed and shining with a faith in the future that would let her see nothing else.

Sam Reeves came over to Cuyler.

'I'm sorry about this, Gene. Me and the other boys did the best we could, but we didn't have much to work with and it had got away to too big a start. I dunno what started it.'

'I do,' said Gene. 'The same skunk who threw phosphorus into the wheat fields, laid a few pieces around here sometime last night. When the sun got warm enough, things began happening. Thanks for everything, Sam—and tell the rest of the boys the same. You did all that was possible and I hope to be able to make it up to you, one of these days.'

'You don't owe me or the rest a damn thing,' said Sam sturdily. 'You've had a rotten deal and me, I'm gettin' damn good and sick of some people in these parts.'

Sam Reeves trudged away and the other men followed him. All except Pierce Pomeroy, who cleared his throat as he came up to Cuyler and spoke with a cold, measured preciseness.

'This is unfortunate, Cuyler. In a way it's your own fault. You grew careless. For a while, I understand, you kept a guard over the corrals here. Then you took it off. This is the result and it alters the business picture considerably. The fact is, a development has come up within the bank which makes it necessary for me to call in a number of outstanding notes. Yours is one of them. Sorry.'

Cuyler whirled on him, fists clenched, big shoulders swung forward. Something that was almost a feral growl broke from Cuyler's lips.

'So! This brings you right out into the open, does it? Don't try and lie to me. Don't turn mealy-mouthed, Pomeroy. You're not sorry. This suits you right down to the ground. For it means you got me over a barrel and you're ready to step in with the knife. But don't make the mistake of getting rough.'

The black, hard curtain over Pierce Pomeroy's eyes seemed to thicken. His face grew pinched and venomous.

'You read the note you signed, Cuyler. A call note it was. Have you the ready cash to cover it?'

'You know damned well I haven't,' Cuyler exploded. 'If I did you wouldn't be coming at me this way. There's a good fifteen hundred dollars' worth of hay in that pile, gone up in smoke. There's several hundred dollars in lumber and labor likewise gone in corrals and feed sheds. So of course I haven't the ready cash to take care of the note. And I know what you're going to say. Which is that in such case you must claim the collateral I put up, my wagons and my mules and other equipment. Well, don't hold your breath until you get 'em. Because you won't!'

'The law,' droned Pomeroy, 'will take care

of that.'

'The law will take care of several things, mister,' was Cuyler's harsh retort. 'There's a joker in this deck and you haven't seen it yet. But you will, and will you be surprised! You see, Pomeroy, I got wise to you just in time. I got my thinking straightened out, finally. Let's consider a picture. Such as a good, soundly established freight line between Capell and Sycamore. I would supply the outfits, do the work, make the fight against the cattle interests. I was to build up these corrals, this wagon camp, get everything sitting pretty. And when all that was done and the plum ripe and ready for picking, you'd move in and drop the ax. Call the note at a time when you knew I couldn't meet it. This fire deal has maybe rushed your hand a little, but it's still the hand you set out to play, right from the first. It made you show your cards. But the joker isn't in your hand. It's in mine.'

'I don't know what you're talking about,' snapped the banker. 'And I've no time to listen to a lot of crazy ravings and threats. I've told you that your note is called. Pay up or I take over.'

There wasn't an ounce of mirth in the hard smile that touched Cuyler's lips.

'You're not calling any note of mine, or the note of any friend of mine, who might, for instance, be Ben Loftus. I'll tell you why. Let me ask you one simple little question. Do you know where Hitch Gower is?'

Pierce Pomeroy went absolutely still. Then his throat worked once or twice before he could speak.

'What's Hitch Gower got to do with it?'

'You should know, Pomeroy. And where is Gower? Right now you'd like mortally to know, wouldn't you? But you don't. And I do. I can put my finger on him any time I want. Hitch Gower's not the sort to take all the blame for anything. In an effort to save his skin he'll talk—and plenty. So now, do you think you're going to call any notes?'

Pomeroy went still again. It was a queer, chilled stillness, masking forces about to explode. It was the last settled pause of a cornered animal about to spring. And the animal did spring.

There was none of Pomeroy's usual measured preciseness in the flashing speed of the hand which darted inside his open coat front, to come away bearing the dark steel of a naked gun. But Gene Cuyler was not to be caught off guard again by Pierce Pomeroy. He matched speed with more speed.

The lunge of his right shoulder was explosive with power. And the drive of his right arm, tipped with a knotted fist, was the dart of a rapier, carrying the smash of a broadsword. Even as Pomeroy got his gun clear of his coat, Cuyler's fist pounded home on the side of the banker's jaw.

The blow spun Pomeroy around, dropped him on his hands and knees. Cuyler leaped for him, reached down and tore the gun from the banker's slack fingers. Then he stepped back and watched Pomeroy stagger to his feet. The latter had to try twice before he made it.

He stood there, weaving and swaying. His mouth sagged half open, a thin line of crimson beginning to dribble from one corner. He was momentarily stupefied with shock. Then the dark blankness of his eyes filled and hardened and seemed to smolder crimson with a wild, deadly hate. He said no word, but seemed to measure Cuyler with a purpose that was all death.

Abruptly he turned and walked away, steady now, his habitual precise stride only slightly jerky from the pressure of the rage that was in him. His arms swung stiffly at his sides, his white hands clenched into knots.

Cuyler watched the banker out of sight then turned away, the tension running out of him to be replaced with a sodden weariness, which was spiritual as well as physical. His thoughts grew dark and moody. Of all the foul things of life, he mused, treachery was the worst, particularly when it was premeditated and coldly schemed. All other frailties of men were but petty meannesses in comparison.

Open enmity was one thing and inevitably a portion of every man's existence, the varying viewpoints of human nature being what they were. But this other thing was sordid and unclean and depressing.

The gurgle of water in the pipes to the troughs drew him. He drank, then scrubbed sweat and grime and soot from his scorched and smarting face. He found burns on his hands and wrists he had not known were there up until now. There were holes in his shirt and jeans, lined with char, where live cinders had settled and left their mark. He wondered if he'd ever get the smell of burning wheat smoke out of his nostrils.

He looked to the south where the sky was sultry with the piled-up stain of smoke. This had been a wicked day, a day of unbridled destruction and had set the stage for an even more savage showdown. He thought of men and of the laws, written and unwritten, which they designed to govern themselves, and of how these laws meant nothing when the forces of men's cruder desires and greeds got the better of them. He could not remember a time when such a sense of draining futility had gripped him....

*　　*　　*

He was feeling a little better when, through a warm, blue twilight, his wagons came rolling back from Sycamore. It was the deathless optimism of youth bounding back from the depths; the indomitable courage and purpose

183

welded into being by a man's dreams. Reaction had come and gone and the old eager vigor had a man's head up once more.

At sight of the smoldering, glowing fodder stack, and of the blackened embers of the feed sheds and corrals, his teamsters gathered around Gene Cuyler with a surge of angry questions.

He quieted them, told them the story. 'And so,' he ended, 'right now we're stuck for hay and corrals, boys. But it's only temporary.'

'That's right, lad,' growled Mike Kenna. 'We were late gettin' in because Jess Petty had twenty ton of good hay hauled in and waitin' for us at Sycamore. Loading that into our wagons took time. But it's in the wagons right now. So our mules won't go hungry just yet. And we can always get by without corrals for a time, so long as we have hay and water.'

Bill Wragg spoke harshly.

'When do we start handing it out instead of taking it, Gene? First Hack Dowd and his outfit. Now this. It ain't like you to take any more without handing some back.'

'We'll hand it back,' said Cuyler in quiet grimness. 'All along I've been hoping that somehow, someway we could work out an agreement with the hostile cattle forces without violence getting out of hand. I realize now that we can't. Certain elements have to be smashed completely before they'll leave us alone. I've done some thinking on it and I'm

184

going to start the first move right away.

'We do no more hauling for a few days. Things are a mess out in the wheat fields and have to be sorted out before our wagons can start rolling again. Which is all right. Gives us a chance to rest up the mules and go over the wagons. In the morning we'll bring down some barbed wire from Gil Saltmarsh's store, set up some posts and build some temporary corrals. Mike, you'll see that guards are set, day and night. Steve, right after supper you and me got a ride to make.'

'You look,' observed Steve, as he and Cuyler went up town, 'like you'd been dragged through hell on your ear and didn't miss all the hot coals on the trip.'

'It was pretty tough going for a while,' nodded Cuyler. 'A new outfit of clothes are in order, I guess. You better slick up a little yourself, for you may see a lady tonight.'

'You mean—Candy?' asked Steve eagerly.

'That's right. The J L is where we're heading.'

The stars were high and bright when Cuyler and Steve Sears rode into the J L headquarters. Ben Loftus' call came harshly from the ranchhouse porch.

'Who rides?'

'Sears and Cuyler,' answered Gene.

'Get down—get down,' growled Loftus testily. 'If I sound mad, it's not at you boys.'

'How's Paula?' asked Cuyler as he climbed

185

the porch steps.

'Tuckered. Candy put her to bed and is taking care of her. By morning she'll be as good as ever. From what she told me it's been quite a day down in the wheat country. While you got considerable of a jolt yourself, didn't you?'

'Considerable,' Cuyler admitted. 'But troubles seem pretty generally spread, Ben. I understand that you got some yourself.'

Ben Loftus had a rifle leaning against the wall beside him. He patted the breech of the weapon.

'See that? Well, that shows I'm expecting most anything to happen the way things are breaking. I'm havin' my eyes opened wider all the time. Teede Hunnewell and Joe Justin seem to think I'm drilling wells and bringing in water for their special benefit.'

'There just isn't any room in this country for those two fellows any longer.' There was a quiet but flat emphasis in Cuyler's tone. 'Paula was telling me about how they'd moved in a mixed herd of Looped H and Broken Bow cattle around your first well. Which is what I rode out to see you about. I'd like to see those cattle in Jim Nickerson's west pasture field.'

'Eh!' ejaculated Loftus. 'What's that? What do you mean?'

Cuyler told him. It made the cattleman get up and stride back and forth excitedly. 'That'll force a wide-open showdown,' he warned.

'Which is what we want, isn't it?' returned

186

Cuyler. 'One thing we've got to make our minds up to. The air has got to be cleared, Ben—once and for all. The issue is plain. It's Hunnewell and Justin—or the rest of us. You're not exempt, yourself. They've shown that by moving in on your water, over your legitimate protest.'

'Probably their idea of gettin' even with me for steppin' out of a senseless and pig-headed fight.'

'Maybe,' nodded Cuyler. 'But it boils down to the same angle they play against everybody, which is: do the way they want you to do, or take the roughing-up treatment they hand out. And if they'll move in on your water, what guarantee have you got that they won't move in on your range, should that hunch hit them?'

Loftus slowed his excited pacing to a thoughtful prowl. 'What you're suggestin' is cattle stealin' on a big scale, Gene.'

'Not necessarily,' Cuyler differed. 'We put the cattle in Nickerson's field and we send word to Hunnewell and Justin. We tell them they can have the stock back by paying for the fire damage they've caused, otherwise we sell the cattle off ourselves to make up for the damage. How a court of law would interpret such a deal I don't know, and I don't care. In the face of what Hunnewell and Justin have done, certainly we've a right to force recompense of some sort. There's no legitimate law in the world which can condemn a man for fighting for his just rights.'

'They got guards watching those cows,' said Loftus. 'Three of 'em. Blaze Doan and Cass Huntoon, who went over to Justin when I fired 'em. And one other regular Broken Bow puncher. Makes me mad as hell every time I think of Doan and Huntoon. I gave them two a good job for a long time. I gave them two or three chances to calm down and behave themselves before I finally fired 'em. Now they turn right around and come against me. Makes a man wonder if there's any sense in givin' anybody a square deal.'

'A certain breed of cats never do recognize a square deal, Ben. But if we can't take care of those three, then we can't take care of anything. And if we're going to take a whirl at this idea, tonight's as good a time as any. How about it?'

Loftus slammed a clenched fist into an open palm.

'It's a deal!'

'Good! We get busy. Steve, you head back for town. Tell Bill Wragg I want him and Zeke Moss and Skeet Yore out at Jim Nickerson's place by midnight. Tell 'em to bring Winchesters. Mike Kenna and the rest of the boys can guard things at the corrals. You get that word passed along, you come back here and wait for me. Ben, you explain to your riders what's in the wind and have them ready. I got a little ride to make. I won't be gone too long.'

Steve, ready to leave, hesitated bashfully, then said, 'Say hello to Candy for me, will you, Mr. Loftus?'

'Sure,' said Loftus. 'Sure I will, son.'

Listening to the receding thump of Steve's pony, Ben Loftus smiled grimly.

'You know, Gene, I think Candy is fonder of that boy than she lets on. Been a big and sudden change in Candy, that I can hardly figure. I admit I've spoiled her to death and that lately she's had me worried considerable. But now of a sudden she's quieted down, turned serious and thoughtful, mainly of others. It ain't like her, but I'm tickled to see it. If I didn't know she's as healthy as a cougar kitten, I'd be afraid she was sick, darned if I wouldn't.'

'Candy's not sick of anything that'll hurt her, Ben,' drawled Cuyler. 'Candy's just growing up, that's all.'

From the J L, Gene Cuyler rode straight to Jim Nickerson's place. Down in the wheat country the night air hung thick and bitter with the smell of burned and blackened acres. And at Nickerson's there was a meeting going on. Abe Pettibone, Mark Travis, Alec McKibbin and several others were there. Wheat men, all. They were a singed, scorched, soot-blackened lot, menacingly grim. Guns of one sort or another were stacked about the room.

'You're just in time, Cuyler,' said Abe

189

Pettibone harshly. 'We're goin' after those damn wheat-burnin' whelps and you and your crowd can buy in, and welcome. We aim to move in on 'em and lay it on the line with hot lead. When it's over with, either they'll be done, or we will.'

'That would be getting off on the wrong foot, Abe,' Cuyler told him gravely. 'They're probably expecting that very reaction and are all set to shoot hell out of you. This is a time to be smarter than they are.'

'Maybe you got a better idea?' growled Mark Travis.

'I think so. If you care to listen?'

'Shoot,' rasped Alec McKibbin. 'We'll listen.'

When Cuyler finished outlining his plan, Jim Nickerson said, 'That's it!'

'The value of the cattle won't near equal what we've lost in burned wheat,' argued Mark Travis.

'I know it won't,' agreed Cuyler. 'But it will still be a lot more than Hunnewell and Justin can afford to lose. On top of that it forces their hand and, best of all, it'll make them come to us instead of us going to them. We'll be the ones who'll be set and waiting and they'll be the ones in the open. Cattle for wheat will be our war cry, and let them try and get the cattle back, by any other means than paying. It's the same kind of medicine they've concocted. We'll see if they can take it.'

190

Mark Travis' eyes began to sharpen as all the possibilities of the plan took hold.

'If it suits the rest, it suits me,' he agreed. 'That's it. Cattle for wheat!'

* * *

They moved away from the J L headquarters right after midnight. Gene Cuyler and Steve Sears, Ben Loftus and four J L riders. They rode a wide and cautious circle, far back into the eastern hills, coming around above and in back of the area where Loftus' first well had been drilled.

'They must have a camp somewhere,' said Cuyler.

'At the head of that little draw which runs south of the well,' volunteered one of the J L punchers briefly.

'They'll be standing watches, of course,' figured Cuyler. 'Which means that two will be in their blankets while the other is out on some lookout point. We'll get the two in the blankets, first. Feel kinda stout, Steve?'

'Damn whistlin'!' declared Steve emphatically. 'Hope I draw Blaze Doan again. That'll give me a chance to finish the chore I was workin' on the night of the dance.'

'You two can't handle the whole job,' objected Ben Loftus. 'If one of those three breaks away and gets word to Hunnewell and Justin ahead of time, this whole thing will blow

191

up in our faces.'

'If one of them gets away on us,' said Gene Cuyler, 'that will be the time for you and your men to go home quietly and not be drawn into things at all, Ben. I figure to hide your participation in this as far as I can. Come on, Steve. We go in on foot.'

Leaving Ben Loftus still growling argument, Gene and Steve struck out, rifles over their arms. Gene moved fast, for they would need every minute of darkness to get the entire job cleaned up before day began to break.

They worked south and around, keeping to the black gloom of gulches as far as possible, never crossing the clear top of a ridge or hill, where their crouched figures might be glimpsed against the stars by someone on watch at a lower altitude. Also, this maneuver enabled them to avoid running into and startling into movement any of the cattle, which were bedded for the night on the open slopes.

'I hope,' mumbled Steve, 'you know where the hell you're goin'.'

'I hope, and think I do,' Gene answered. 'Save your breath.'

Cuyler listened even more than he looked, for there was a night wind flowing across these lonely folded hills. And finally he heard the sound he wanted, which was the whir of spinning windmill blades and the measured clank of a pump rod sliding up and down. With the windmill located, it was easy to find the gulch to the south.

They went into the head of it, low-crouched and cautious. The breeze, running up the gulch, brought them the smell of horses, of stale fire embers and the odor of cold bacon grease in a frying pan. But no scent of tobacco smoke, which was what Cuyler was worried about and wanted to locate. For that would have meant locating whoever was standing this dark, chill watch.

He led the way, inching down gulch, then froze to immobility as a harsh voice lashed out.

'Stay right there! Another move and you get it!'

Blaze Doan's voice! Blaze Doan standing guard. They had crept right up on him, but the surprise was his, not theirs. He had them— cold! Here could be complete failure of their carefully laid plan.

Doan's voice came at them again, hard, wary and alert.

'Who is it? Speak up—quick!'

Before Gene Cuyler could think of or give an answer, he heard the stir of Steve Sears in movement behind him, heard Steve grunt softly in a gesture of violent effort. He heard the swish of something lashing through the air above and past him, something which struck something else with a solid crunch, then dropped to earth with a metallic clank, and then something else falling in a heavy, sodden way.

193

Steve went past Cuyler like a projectile from a gun, and he was mumbling triumphantly.

'Got him! Now for the others. Make it fast, Gene!'

There was nothing else to do now but follow this wild kid in his headlong rush down the gulch. Just ahead Cuyler heard a sleepy voice mumbling cursing questions. This broke off in a snarl of alarm and a tangle of conflict as Steve Sears launched himself on the blanket-muffled speaker.

Cuyler thought, 'The kid must have eyes like a cat or an owl. I can't see a damn thing!'

Not seeing, he tripped and fell over a heaving, stirring bulk on the ground. He rolled over, got his feet under him and dove back at that bulk, just in time to get his hands on a figure that was shedding blankets and startled curses at an equal rate of speed.

Cuyler took a wildly swinging but rawhide-hard fist in the face as a price for the chance to get in close with his man. Then it became strictly dog eat dog.

They spun around, tangled their feet in blankets and went down. Cuyler took a driving knee in the stomach which didn't do him a bit of good, as it drained strength and breath from him. The fellow guessed his advantage, dropped his weight across Cuyler and held him so, while slugging blindly with both fists. Some of these punches missed but others landed, and Cuyler knew he had to do something besides be on the receiving end of this business, or one of those punches would connect squarely and it would be all over.

He gave over trying to shield himself from the mauling fists, drove both his hands up, fingers spread and gripping. He found the fellow's chin, his throat. He sank his fingers in, pushed his arms to full, straight length.

The fellow jerked and tore, trying to pull free, while at the same time keeping his hammering fists going. It was brutal, wicked, primitive stuff, like two animals locked in mortal combat. The fellow's breath took on a thin, dragging whistling as he tried to get air into his tortured lungs. Abruptly he gave off swinging his fists, grabbed at Cuyler's wrists and tried to wrench clear of Cuyler's deadly grip.

This was the break Cuyler had been waiting for. He arched his back against the earth, threw all he had into a rolling surge. It did the trick, throwing his opponent over and down, but it tore his grip loose. Cuyler scrambled to his knees, dove after his man anew.

He could hear the fellow rolling and lunging down gulch, trying to get away. But Cuyler caught up with him, got an arm about his neck, pulled his head in tight and clubbed a chopping right fist at the fellow's temple. Again and again he smashed that fist home before the fellow weakened. Twice more Cuyler used his hammering fist, and now, finally, the fellow was limp and senseless.

Cuyler hunkered back, something almost like a groan breaking through clenched teeth. It hadn't been too long, this struggle, but the sheer ferocity of it had used up an enormous well of energy. Cuyler felt wrenched and beaten all over. Breath sobbed from his lungs and he mopped blindly at his bleeding lips. He managed to mumble a single hoarse word.

'Steve?'

'All right here,' was Steve's sturdy answer. 'I got all the water wrung out of this one. What you been doing?'

That irrepressible kid! Cuyler knew a crazy, wild desire to laugh. But he didn't. He spat blood from his mouth before answering.

'Been having a damn rough ride. Not sure if it was a man or a bear I tangled with. But he's quiet, now. Tell me—what the devil did you throw at Doan?'

'My rifle. It was our only chance outside of shootin' him, for he'd have been throwing lead our way in another second. I can think of lots of things I'd rather have thrown at me than a rifle, flailing round and around. I saw a barkeep clear a whole saloon doorway one time, by throwin' a sawed-off shotgun like that.'

'You might have missed him.'

'Yeah, I might. But I didn't. A whirlin' rifle takes in quite a chunk of territory and I had him pretty well located by his voice. I better go take a look at him and see what the damage is.'

Steve went scrambling back up the gulch, to stop presently and lean over something on the ground, scratching a match to get light for a better look. Cuyler was content to stay just as he was, waiting for the whirling fogs to leave his brain and strength to seep back into his racked and shaken body.

This day—! One long battle it seemed to have been. Against fire and against men. Cuyler wondered how far a man's strength and will could carry him without rest. He pushed aside this weakening thought, crawled over to the man he'd subdued, searched for and found a match and used the meagre light of it.

Cass Huntoon had been his man, heavy, burly and brutal. A bear of a man, true enough, and even now shaking off the effects of Cuyler's battering fist. Cuyler pushed him face down on the ground and held him so with a knee between his shoulders, while calling to Steve.

'Bring a rope, kid! Must be some in their camp gear.'

Steve found some and brought it and Gene set to tying Huntoon up.

'Same medicine for the others, kid. Get at it!'

'Doan won't need any,' Steve said. 'My rifle hit him right across the side of the face and head. He's out cold and from the looks of him, will stay that way.'

'No matter. Tie him up. These three got to

keep right here for hours. We still got plenty to do.'

CHAPTER TEN

GRIM TALLY

It was a big drift of cattle that moved across the plains through the darkness. It was inevitable that, in making a gather under these conditions, a lot of the cattle would be J L stuff, but these would be cut out and headed back into the hills when it got light enough to see clearly.

In the first chill light of dawn they massed the cattle before Jim Nickerson's west pasture field and set about sifting Looped H and Broken Bow cows through the pasture gate, while cutting J L stock back. They worked with a driving speed and the chore was finished just before sunup. Cuyler turned to Ben Loftus.

'You and your boys skim along home now, Ben. The rest of this is up to us who took the licking by fire.'

'I don't like to pull out just when the going is due to get real rough,' the cattleman growled.

'You got Paula and Candy to think of,' Cuyler reminded. 'Besides, the real ruckus is none of your affair. You helped move Hunnewell and Justin cattle away from your

198

water, which makes you even with them there. You've done your share. We could never have pulled this without your help.'

Loftus looked Cuyler over gravely, then spoke gruffly.

'The first time I met up with you I knew there was rawhide in you. You're a tough hombre, Gene.'

Cuyler's beaten features pulled into a wryly clumsy grin.

'I don't feel tough. I feel like I'd been dragged through a keyhole, against the grain. It's rough world, Ben. I'll be seeing you.'

Loftus started to rein away, hesitated, his gruffness deepening.

'Take care of yourself, boy. This country and certain people in it, can't afford to lose you. Good luck!'

With Loftus and his riders gone, Cuyler went over to Jim Nickerson, who sat the fence by the gate.

'How did they count out, Jim?'

'I made it a hundred and ninety-four, running about half and half of Looped H and Broken Bow brands.'

'Which represents a chunk of money Hunnewell and Justin can hardly afford to pass up,' Cuyler nodded. 'This will bring action. Get your guards out. I got another ride to make, but I'll be back in time for the fireworks.'

Cuyler wondered which was the more weary, himself or his horse as he rode at a logy, shuffling jog back across the brightening plain and up into the hills beyond. He felt all soggy and loose, with a constant necessity of straightening his shoulders, lest the sag of them drag him completely out of the saddle. Hunger gnawed at him but that was the least of his physical miseries. Sleep was what he needed.

But sleep would have to wait. Forces had been set in motion across these plains and hills which from now on would mount rapidly to a crashing crescendo. Issues born of greed and hate had snowballed to a point where something had to give, one way or another. This was war, with the smoke of the final battles already seeping against the wide sky.

This chore he was now about could have been taken care of by Ben Loftus, except that it would have definitely tied Loftus in with the cattle deal. And while Hunnewell and Justin might later put two and two together and arrive at the correct answer, it was just as well to keep them guessing at that angle as long as possible.

Cuyler found that he and Steve Sears had done a good job of tying up. Blaze Doan, Cass Huntoon and the other Broken Bow hand lay just as he and Steve had left them. Cuyler's first move was to collect every weapon he could find and stick it in a gunny sack tied to his saddle. Then he loosed the bounds of the three riders and lined them up at the muzzle of his rifle.

'You've signed on with a losing hand,' he

told them curtly. 'The wheat men and me called a little shot of our own, last night. You can take this news back to Justin and Hunnewell. Tell them that we got a hundred and ninety-four head of Looped H and Broken Bow cattle in Jim Nickerson's west pasture. If Hunnewell and Justin want those cows back they can have them by paying for the fire damage they've done to the wheat men and me. If they don't want to pay, why then we'll peddle the cows ourselves and realize what we can on the deal. We'll keep on at the same kind of business until we come out even. And if Hunnewell and Justin don't like our idea, well, the next move is up to them. Your horses are yonder and there are your saddles. Git!'

There was no fight left in them. They went, surly but subdued. Blaze Doan staggered a little as he moved, a sick man for, as Steve had said, he had taken the full impact of Steve's thrown rifle across the side of his face. His mouth hung slightly open as though his jaw had been broken or the muscles of his face paralyzed.

Cuyler went slowly into his own saddle, wondering at the effort it took. Of its own accord his horse moved off along the gulch and over to where Ben Loftus' windmill spun in bright newness in the sunlight. At the trough the horse plunged its muzzle deep and drank thirstily. A line of J L cattle were already coming in around a hill slope, cattle that had not been picked up in the dark drive of the early morning, now drawn by the lure of the bright sparkling water that poured from the trough pipe.

Where the seepage of the overflow of the trough spread its damp darkness, the first green of fresh sprouting grass made a sharp contrast to the tawniness of the summer-dried grass about it. Above the seepage blackbirds fluttered, a pair of killdeer lilted and small grass finches darted in and out.

The sun, earth and water. These things spelled life. For men, only the sun was free to all. Over the rest men knew contest, battle.

Gene Cuyler reined away, down the slope, his mood darkly brooding. His face was craggy, the angles of it sharp and hard-drawn, thinned by fatigue and strain. He had the strange feeling that he was no longer his own master, charting his own trail and moving along it of his own volition. Now he was a harried slave to events. A man might have had a plan of straightforward simplicity, involving nothing more difficult than hard work and a reasonable amount of tenacity. Given these, fair success was assured. That was the theory of the thing. But nothing was ever that simple, it seemed.

Always there were the plans of other men, running athwart his own. Some of these offered no cause for contest or argument or battle. But there was always someone who stood squarely in the trail, claiming it for his own alone, blocking off all others who would use it. And when a man met up with that sort of thing he was left with but one of two choices. He weakened and quit—or he went ahead.

To do the first meant complete ruin of the future. If he did the second it meant battle which, once started, had to be fought to the finish regardless of cost. And no man ever came out of such battle the same as he was when he entered it. Even if he came out victor, there were certain penalties exacted. He would be inevitably older in spirit and touched by the bitter acid of cynicism.

Maybe it was an ordered test which life exacted of every man for the mere privilege of living. Maybe it was the working of an ancient and all-wise law calculated to define the strong from the weak and so build soundly for all the measureless future. But there were times when, faced with the certainty of battle and the equal certainly of its cost, that a man might know doubts of the worth of that future.

Cuyler shook himself, trying to get out from under the weight of this mood. For while it was given to man that he be able to reason, that very gift could lead him down gloomy mental trails where the bright flavor of life seemed all but lost.

Cuyler built a cigarette and was grateful for the tang of it in his lungs and the purely physical bite of it across his battered lips. He eased himself a little in the saddle and rode the miles down across the plains.

*   *   *

A hand on Gene Cuyler's shoulder urged him to wakefulness. Drugged with fatigue on returning to Jim Nickerson's place, he had sprawled on the earth by the pasture gate and knew sleep almost instantly. Now it was Steve Sears shaking him.

'They're here, Gene—and it looks like the business. They're sending a man in.'

Cuyler got to his feet, shook himself, blinked sleep-dulled eyes. The sun was well over. It was mid-afternoon, of a day that had grown particularly hot. In the distance a group of riders waited while one of their number came in toward the pasture gate at a steady jog.

Jim Nickerson, Abe Pettibone and Alec McKibbin stood leaning on the gate, rifles over their arms. Nickerson's voice was a quiet growl.

'That's Hunnewell ridin' in. We'll let you do the talkin', Gene. Don't bargain an inch with him. I can see where things have been building right up to this point. It had to come, and now that we've taken our stand, this is it!'

Teede Hunnewell rode stiffly in his saddle, hitched a trifle to one side to favor his healing leg. He brought his horse to a halt ten yards from the gate, let his glance run over the cattle

204

in the pasture, then brought it to the men guarding the gate. His florid, big-nosed face was flushed with anger.

'You're a flock of damn cow thieves,' he rapped harshly. 'You got ten minutes to open that gate and chouse those cows back on to clear range. Otherwise we come and get them—and you! That is my last word.'

'Doan and Huntoon and that other rider of Justin's brought you our terms, didn't they?' answered Cuyler. 'Well, the terms still stand—and they won't change. Better think everything over plenty careful before you start something you can't stop. You and Justin have pushed things to a showdown and right here and on this issue we make our stand.'

Hunnewell looked at him, hard; red hate in his eyes.

'Biggest mistake I ever made in my life was not runnin' that chicken-livered Loftus out of the picture and then lettin' the boys tromp you to death the day they gave you that goin' over in town. Yeah, I should have let them kill you, Cuyler, then and there. Well, it's a mistake that'll be corrected this day.'

Cuyler shrugged.

'Words and the act don't always jibe, Hunnewell. You know, it's hard to figure out men like you and Justin. And you're wrong about Ben Loftus. He's not chicken-livered. He's got more real nerve than you and Justin put together. Ben had nerve enough to admit

205

he'd been wrong and take steps to correct things generously. But you and Justin—! You beat up people, you burn their wheat. You rant and rave and threaten. And then squeal like hogs under a gate when you get some of your own medicine. You think only a man in a saddle has any rights in this world. There's an awful lot you don't understand about your fellow man, Hunnewell. Well, you know our terms. Cattle for wheat. Now, what about it?'

'Yeah, Hunnewell—what about it?' put in Abe Pettibone. 'Some of us just got through watchin' a season of slaving work go up in smoke, in fire that your crowd started. We've taken every damn bit of persecution from you and Justin that we're goin' to. Now, damn you—put up or shut up!'

Hunnewell's look became almost choleric. 'Damn, sod-bustin' fools! Let's hear you argue after you're dead!'

He spun his horse and rode away, back to the group of riders who waited for him just out of long rifle range of the pasture gate. When he reached them the riders bunched around him for a minute or two, then spread out in a thin line and began moving slowly in.

Presently far, flat echoes of rifle shots began to whip across the world and then there were bullets kicking up dust, well short of the pasture fence, to bounce and snap and whine away overhead in ricochet. Gradually the riders drew closer and the bullets likewise.

Gene Cuyler turned to Nickerson and the others.

'Spread out and get down on the ground,' he ordered. 'And save your lead. Let them waste theirs.'

The feeling came to Cuyler that this thing was sour, somehow. While he realized fully the furious anger burning in Teede Hunnewell, he could not figure the man as having lost all sense of balance and judgement. To keep on advancing in the wide open, as he and his men were doing, was to invite certain defeat. Open targets as they were, they and their horses would most surely be cut down, once they got within fair rifle range of these defenders of the pasture and the cattle, men who were now flattened close to the earth and offering a very minimum of target area to the cattle crowd. No, it didn't make sense.

Bill Wragg must have seen things this same way, for he moved over beside Cuyler.

'This is phony, Gene. They could fool around out there for a week wasting lead, and not doing us a lick of harm or themselves a lick of good. I got the feelin' that all they really want is just to keep us lookin' that way. I'm rememberin' this ain't the only side to this field and that the southwest corner of it ain't more'n a lick and a spit from the willow thickets along Bench Crick. Also, I keep askin' myself— where's Joe Justin? So, if we keep watchin' too long an' hard this way, we may find our real trouble comin' in out of those willow thickets.'

Cuyler nodded, smiling bleakly.

'You're a fox, Bill. You've given me the answer I was looking for. Get Skeet Yore and Zeke Moss and come on.'

Cuyler went over to Jim Nickerson and explained. Nickerson nodded vehemently.

'That's wise. Go along. We'll watch that crowd out front.'

They went back through the pasture, the cattle swinging and milling away and about, already restless and edgy because of the wailing ricochets of slugs coming in from Hunnewell and his crowd up front.

Someone moved up beside Cuyler. It was Steve Sears. Cuyler spoke sharply.

'You get back with Nickerson, Steve. Skeet and Bill and Zeke and me can handle things on this end.'

There was a hard, bright glint in Steve's eyes. He shook his head.

'You're my real gang. You wouldn't be comin' back here unless you figgered this was where the real danger lay. And in a showdown I travel with my own crowd.'

'But I made a promise to Candy Loftus about you,' Cuyler protested. 'You—'

'I'm stayin' right with you,' cut in Steve. 'You and Candy mean well, but in a deal like this a man draws his own cards. I'm drawin' mine.'

Bill Wragg's voice lifted in a yell of alarm.

208

'Watch yourselves, boys. Here they come!'

They were still a good hundred yards from the rear fence of the pasture when what Bill Wragg had figured would happen, did happen. A group of riders came racing out of the creek bottoms. They fanned out swiftly and tore in on the fence, riding silently until they saw Cuyler and his men working their way through the cattle. Then they began to shoot.

Right in front of him, Gene Cuyler saw a clod of pasture sod bounce into the air and the whine of the ricocheting bullet was a banshee screech close over his head. Another slug snapped by, to thud solidly into living flesh behind him. A cow critter bawled forlornly and collapsed.

'Down!' yelled Bill Wragg. 'Down on the ground!'

They flattened out, a position that became more hair-raising by the second. For the cattle, now fully stirred by the violence erupting on both sides of them, began racing and milling wildly in all directions. Deadly guns out there beyond the fence and on this side the strong possibility of being trampled to death at any second.

The charge of the riders carried them right up to the fence and Cuyler glimpsed one of them leaning from his saddle, reaching for the fence with a pair of wire cutters. Between two of the posts a top wire twanged sharply and whipped back in a vicious curl.

So that, thought Cuyler, was to be the real strategy of the cattle forces. Hunnewell and his party to hold attention up front, while these riders were to cut the back fence, open it up and let the harried, milling cattle through and out into open country, leaving the wheat men and himself holding an empty sack.

'Drive 'em away from that fence!' yelled Cuyler.

On his right Zeke Moss got to one knee, to see better and shoot better. A bullet slapped. Zeke's head jerked and he went down in a loose heap. Skeet Yore cursed savagely and dropped the rider with the wire cutters, right across the second wire, where he hung limply at the waist, like an empty sack.

Off to the left another cut wire twanged and Cuyler glimpsed a second rider at work, already grabbing with his cutters at the second wire. Cuyler swung his rifle, but a frantic cow, charging by, blotted out the target. Bill Wragg's rifle snarled and when the cow got by, Cuyler could see the rider sliding from his saddle.

This punishment was a little too grim for the cattle crowd. Resistance at this end of the pasture was something they hadn't counted on. They gave back, fleeing into the willows.

Skeet Yore called harshly.

'Grab hold, somebody! Help me with Zeke. We got to get him and ourselves over to that fence or we get trampled by these damned

210

cattle. Quick! Before that crowd gets set to come at us again.'

The only reason they made it to the fence was because the cattle, racing and whirling about them, gave them some cover against the vengeful riders. One critter, tearing at full speed right across in front of them, turned a complete arc, landing with sodden heaviness, neck broken by a bullet intended for Cuyler or one of his men.

It was Steve Sears who was helping Skeet Yore with Zeke Moss, and there was a betraying looseness about Zeke as they pulled him along that set a cold emptiness in Cuyler's stomach. He knew, without closer examination, that Zeke Moss was dead.

Zeke Moss, lank, slow-speaking, good-natured. Wanting nothing better of life than the freedom and still peace of the open road, with a string of patient mules plodding out the miles ahead and a freight wagon rolling underneath him. The simple, humble wants of a simple, humble man. And here, in this harried field, he had found death....

Cuyler's glance probed the creek willows with bleak intentness. He had flattened out behind a fence post, with Bill Wragg, Skeet Yore and Steve Sears doing likewise. The posts offered scant cover, yet it was a man's instinct to use any shelter available, even if that shelter was more illusion than fact. Lead rained at them. A slug tore a gust of splinters from

211

Gene's post and the flying wood particles stung his neck and the side of his face.

Bill Wragg and Skeet Yore were shooting steadily, searching the willows with their lead, and both were mean men with a Winchester. The cover of the willows was not too thick, once a man set himself to probe it carefully, and Cuyler glimpsed mounted figures whirling and darting beyond the leafy shroud. Several times he caught almost clear glances of dodging targets, but never long enough to swing his rifle into line. Yet he saw enough on two different occasions to identify the men. One was Cass Huntoon and the other Joe Justin.

A grim fact pounded its way through Cuyler's mind. As things lay now the cattle forces had the advantage. Once they cooled off enough to master their instinct of sticking to their saddles, once they started to fight on foot, where the thicker growth of the base of the willow thickets would give them complete coverage, the cattle forces would have all the edge. From that thick cover they could pick off Cuyler and his men at their leisure. So Cuyler knew what had to be done and he set about doing it.

He writhed forward under the wire of the fence and sent his call to the others.

'Keep 'em plenty busy. I'm going out there!'

Steve Sears yelled, 'No! Not that, you wild fool. You won't have a chance. Gene! Come back here or I go with you!'

Bill Wragg understood. He saw the need of just what Gene Cuyler had set out to do.

'Stay put, kid!' he growled at Steve. 'It's our only chance. One man working on them right in the willows is worth a dozen where we are. Spread some lead! Gene'll make it!'

Steve's answer was to squirm under the wire and start crawling after Cuyler.

Bill Wragg cursed helplessly as he plugged fresh ammunition through the loading gate of his rifle and, with Skeet Yore to help, coldly and savagely searched the willow thickets with bitter lead.

Out there a horseman glimpsed the crawling, scrambling figures of Gene Cuyler and Steve Sears. He yelled a warning, fought his nervous, plunging mount to a stand, rose high in his stirrups and pulled down on Gene Cuyler.

Cass Huntoon had hardly hoped for a chance like this, not at point-blank range and with the man he hated above all others out there in the open. It was a chance he meant to make the most of. He delayed a split second to make absolutely sure of the shot. All the brute in him was rampant, now. His teeth were bared, his heavy face twisted in a snarl of concentration.

Bill Wragg's rifle chopped another wicked echo. Cass Huntoon swayed far back in his saddle before the power of some invisible might. His face went slack, his rifle slithered

213

from his hands. He half turned in a slow, wheeling fall. He landed heavily and was still.

Gene Cuyler saw none of this. For here was an ancient cattle trail, coming into the creek at an angle. And there was a low-cut bank which the trail broke through in a deep and narrow furrow which bulwarked a man fully. Cuyler dove into this and gathered himself for the final dash. Out there, not ten yards distant across a stretch of sand and gravel, lay the masking shroud of the willows.

Dust drifted down across Cuyler's sprawled figure, coming from in back of him. He jerked his head around and saw Steve Sears stretched out behind him.

'Steve! You crazy fool kid! I told you to stay back with Bill and Skeet.'

'I'm here,' answered Steve. 'There's the willows, yonder. Let's get into 'em. We're wastin' time, and we can't do Bill and Skeet no good belly down in this groove. Let's go!'

It was useless to argue. Steve was where he was and that was all there was to it. They could not stay where they were and be of any use in this fight. And they couldn't go back. Cuyler realized he was drenched with sweat and some of it slimed down his forehead and stung his eyes. He blinked this aside, measured distance ahead, gathered himself and raced out across the stretch of gravel.

He found himself counting his lunging strides. Five—six—seven—! He literally dove

214

the rest of the way, and that sudden, lunging lift was all that got him clear of a bullet that came smashing at him from the side—from his right.

The gun that threw the slug blared from close in and Cuyler, twisting his head, saw the darkly malignant figure of Joe Justin crouched under the lee of the out bank some fifteen yards above where the cattle trail angled in. Justin, cursing because he'd missed, was jacking another shell into his rifle.

Gene Cuyler, thinking of Steve Sears coming across the clear in front of Justin, opened his mouth to yell warning, then held the shout back because he knew it would do no good. Steve would be making his dash by this time....

The spot where Cuyler ended his desperate dive was where the creek, during some past freshet stage, had gouged a shallow pothole from around the base of the willow clump. Cuyler landed skidding and rolling into this. But he drove himself up desperately, rifle pushed ahead of him.

He did not sight. He had no time. He merely pointed the weapon and shot. The report of his gun and that of Joe Justin's blended into one. Joe Justin fell over against the cut bank and slid down. There was the clank of metal as Steve Sears' rifle dropped on the gravel bar. And Cuyler, turning, saw Steve hunched and writhing over it.

There was no movement in Joe Justin. Cuyler went back into the open of the gravel bar.

'Steve! Kid—!'

Steve had quit his struggling. Cuyler, heart in his mouth, turned the kid over. Steve's face was white, his teeth set, but he managed a ghost of his old irrepressible grin.

'Hi, Boss! Widest damn stretch of gravel I ever tried—to—cross—!'

Steve slumped and was still.

Cuyler half dragged, half carried him over to the temporary security of the pothole under the willows. The right side and front of Steve's shirt was soggy with blood. Cuyler tore the shirt apart with taut, powerful hands. The bullet had struck high up on the right side, driven across at an angle, and come out near the center of the chest. That chest was still lifting and falling with the breath of life as Gene Cuyler worked to stanch the flow of blood with remnants of Steve's shirt.

The far call of Bill Wragg's voice carried in.

'Gene—Gene! You all right—?'

Cuyler's answer was mechanical, dry and harsh with dread.

'All right! But Steve's hit—!'

It hardly seemed possible that anyone could have got from the pasture fence to the creek as fast as Bill Wragg came. And Skeet Yore was with him.

These old-timers knew what to do without

waste of words. Bill Wragg dropped down to help Cuyler, while Skeet Yore, intent and deadly began scouting the willow thickets.

Gene Cuyler became suddenly aware of a great and breathless silence hanging over the world. Gunfire, near and far, had ceased.

'It's over, Bill,' he blurted. 'But Steve—just at the end—'

'I think so,' said Bill gruffly. 'We've licked 'em. The kid—well, I've seen lesser men get over worse. One of us has got to give up his shirt.'

Cuyler had his off first. They tore it in strips, managed crude bandages. They had just finished when Skeet Yore came prowling back. He walked over to Joe Justin, who had not moved, looked at the fallen cattleman for a moment then came over to the pothole.

'We used 'em rough,' he said somberly. 'But they asked for it. Justin's done for and there's a couple more back yonder. Huntoon and another. And two more up at the fence. The kid—?'

'Hard hit, but doin' pretty good,' said Bill Wragg sturdily. 'Darned gay young whelp—I'm plenty fond of him. Bring my rifle, Skeet.'

Bill Wragg, wiry and tough as rawhide, stooped, picked Steve Sears up in his arms and headed back for the pasture.

CHAPTER ELEVEN

GRAY INTERLUDE

A spring wagon, padded thick with wheat straw and blankets, scudded swiftly for Capell. Driving it was Bill Wragg. In back lay Steve Sears and one of Jim Nickerson's farm hands. Skeet Yore had gone on ahead by horseback to round up a doctor and have him ready.

Back at the Nickerson ranch men went about a grim and somber chore. Jim Nickerson spoke gravely to Gene Cuyler.

'When that ruckus broke at the lower end of the pasture, Hunnewell and his crowd came in on the dead run, throwing all the lead they could. Hunnewell was the first to go down and the rest broke and rode for it. But they left Mark Travis dead and Manny Leone with a smashed shoulder.' Nickerson's tone went weary and bitter. 'A steep price all around for the mere privilege of the luckier of us to go on living. Even for Hunnewell and Justin I could have wished something better. I wonder if this land will be more fertile now, for the blood that's gone into it?'

Gene Cuyler felt a million years old, all dry and harsh and drained inside. His very thoughts seemed stiff and unnatural. He borrowed a shirt from Jim Nickerson, glanced once more at the line of silent, blanketed figures lying under an open-fronted shed, climbed slowly into his saddle and rode away, heading for the J L headquarters.

He wondered vaguely if he'd ever know the old flavor of life again, breathe the sweetness of the earth and the far purity of the night and take this given bounty with the old eagerness. He doubted that he would, for though this thing was over for some, it was not over for him. Insistent on his mind was the grinding conviction that he was foredoomed to more of the piled-up fury that came out of the dark recesses of men's passions and plotting.

The sheer hell of it was, he could not get away from it. The time to stop a thing was before you ever started it. But once started, and with trusted and well-liked friends and companions having paid the supreme price, why then you had to go along to the finish, whatever it might be. Else you would have the ghost of their sacrifice forever leering at your shoulder.

He was haggard and stony-faced when he rode up to the J L. He had not realized how much of the day had slipped away. Already the sun was drowning in its own glory beyond the Brushy Hills and the supper gong of this ranch was jangling its call.

Ben Loftus came toward the ranchhouse from the corrals, saw Cuyler and hastened over. He took one glance at Cuyler's face and

219

said, 'Something's done with—and it was bad!'

Cuyler nodded slowly.

'Teede Hunnewell and Joe Justin are done for, Ben. So's Cass Huntoon and some more. On our side we lost Zeke Moss and Mark Travis. And Steve Sears hurt wicked. The doctor should be working on him in Capell by this time. I thought Candy—might want to know.'

Loftus stood still for a moment, his eyes clouding. His voice went gruff and growling.

'It's worse than I thought it could be. I'll call—Candy.'

She came out, yellow head glinting in a last sun ray. Her eyes grew dark and big and stricken as she listened, then went blind with tears. She turned to her father.

'I'm going to town, Dad.'

'Of course,' said Loftus gently. 'I want you to. And Paula with you. That boy will need nursing.'

Cuyler helped Loftus hook up the buckboard. The girls came out, Candy at a run, whimpering with impatience and a rising dread. At sight of Gene Cuyler's face, Paula Juilliard caught her breath, came close to him and spoke softly and with the depth of great wisdom.

'No, Gene! Don't look like that. It's not your fault. Such things are written.'

'It was an idea of mine that forced the showdown,' Cuyler told her. 'For that, I'm to blame. I'll never forget that.'

The buckboard raced away into the first forming tide of a powder blue twilight. Ben Loftus dropped a hand on Cuyler's arm.

'Paula's right,' he said. 'This thing was building up before you ever came to Vaca Plains, boy. Other men poured the first drop of poison, and I was one of them, to my everlasting discredit. Come on. You need some supper.'

The glow of his still-smoldering hay pile guided Gene Cuyler back to Capell. Bill Wragg was there to meet him, knew the question nagging at Gene's mind and answered it.

'Steve's doin' as well as can be expected. The doc ain't makin' promises either way, but he don't seem too gloomy. The kid's young and strong and clean and such things mean a lot in a case like this. Those two girls are on hand and doc's glad about that. Here, I'll put up your bronc.'

Mike Kenna came up out of the dark.

'You've been down a hard stretch, lad,' he said kindly. 'So get away for a rest. Yet before you go I would tell you of the fellow who was hanging around some today, looking things over. He spoke of you when I questioned him and said his business would be with you.'

'Was his name Cade Booker?' asked Gene.

'I don't know,' answered Mike. 'He would not give it when I asked. He was a dark-skinned fellow and, while I'm not of a

221

suspicious nature, it struck me that there was something almost secretive about him.'

'It wasn't Booker,' decided Cuyler. 'Well, I'll probably bump into him—later. Thanks, Mike.'

At the hotel Sam Reeves spoke from the darkness of the porch, where he sat smoking.

'Doc Padgett just left, Gene—after droppin' in for another look at the kid. When he left, doc was whistlin'. I've knowed doc for a long time and I know that when he's whistlin' he ain't worried. The girls are gonna take turns sittin' up the night with Steve.'

Cuyler took a chair beside the hotelkeeper, built a smoke.

'I feel better,' he said simply. 'It's been a rough ride, Sam.'

'I've watched it comin',' mused Reeves. 'There'll always be a few wise men and plenty of fools in the world. Hunnewell and Justin were fools. Nothing stands still. The world moves and changes and a smart man sets his sights according. Hunnewell and Justin wouldn't do that, so the world rolled 'em under. It's always been that way, I reckon. There's always some who won't either get in step or get out of the way. We don't like to see these things, Gene. But they do come along.'

Cuyler had his smoke out, then hitched stiffly to his feet. 'I just thought of something I'd like to do,' he said. 'I won't explain, for you'll think I'm crazy, Sam.'

He went quietly to his room, got soap and a towel and rolled some fresh clothes into a bundle. He went out of the hotel the back way and cut across from town through the dark. The night was warm and out here he had the world to himself and all was still and peaceful. Five minutes' walk brought the spread of willow thickets lifting before him and the soft murmur of running water. Here was another part of Bench Creek, looping lazily from north to south.

Below the riffle a pool spread, spangled with star reflections. Cuyler stripped, stepped into the cool caress of the water. He soaped himself from head to foot, dove and swam and the water was a touch of benediction across his beaten, weary body.

A heron, disturbed in its roost by Cuyler's soft splashing, lifted on invisible wings, its unmusical protest drifting down as it flapped away. Cuyler swam to the head of the pool, turned on his back and floated the length of the pool on the soft, lazy push of the current drift.

Yes, this was what he needed, this peace and the close embrace of elemental things. Simple things. The sweet silence of night and the soft chuckling of free waters.

He felt his muscles loosen and relax. The harsh, grinding inner strain left him. He filled his lungs with the cool, damp odors of the creek, which removed all taint of smoke. Smoke of burning wheat fields. Smoke of even more sinister origin—gun smoke—

He swam over to his gear, stood on clean sand and toweled himself dry. He pulled on the fresh clothes and headed back for town. Weariness was still upon him, but it was a soft, relaxed weariness, now. He went into the hotel quietly, sought his room and slept like a log.

Sunlight was slanting through the window of his room when he got up. He moved with renewed vigor. Shaving, he found, was a painful process when a man's face still bore the bruises and cuts of physical combat. But he managed it and saw that his eyes were clear and bright with restored strength. Hunger was a live thing inside him.

He picked up his hat and was about to leave the room, when a thought struck him, turning him back to the bed, on a corner post of which hung his belt and holstered six-gun. This, he thought gravely, was day, and realities were realities in the light of it. He did not strap the belt on, but lifted the gun from the holster and slipped it down inside the waist band of his jeans, well back on the left side, where the hang of his denim jumper would cover it. He was remembering that the known casualties of yesterday's battle did not include Gatt Ivance.

There was one other late diner breakfasting at the Elite. A man with a thin, swarthy face, marked chiefly by a pair of black eyes, beady and sharp and deep lines of dissipation about the mouth. Cuyler felt the fellow's studying

224

glance, and, as Cuyler took his seat at a corner table, he saw the fellow hail the passing waitress and ask something of her.

When the waitress had taken Cuyler's order, the swarthy man came over to Cuyler's table.

'You,' he said, a slurring note in his voice, 'are Cuyler?'

Gene nodded. 'That's right. Something you wanted?'

The fellow pulled up a chair and sat down.

'I am Pico Rodriquez. I have been looking for you. There is a question of property rights we must discuss.' His glance met Cuyler's, then slid away.

'I'm listening,' said Cuyler briefly.

'At the south of town,' said Rodriquez. 'Those corrals where you kept your mules, the land your wagon camp is on, the old adobe building—that property is mine. It came down to me from the time of my great-grandfather. Word came to me that the property was up for sale to recover back taxes. I came to take care of those taxes and reclaim my property. Also to collect the money you owe me for the use you have had of it.'

'Thoughtful of you,' remarked Cuyler, drily sarcastic.

Rodriquez flushed under his swarthiness. 'I will also consider selling the property—for ten thousand dollars.'

Cuyler laughed.

'It's not worth any reasonable part of ten

thousand dollars. Even if it were I wouldn't pay it. As for claiming I owe you any money for the use I've had of it, that's pretty far-fetched. Plenty of others have used the layout, long before I ever saw this part of the country. You calculate to dun them, too?'

Rodriquez twitched his shoulders in a faint shrug.

'I know nothing of others. I know only that I find you here, using property that is not yours. You will pay me a fair rental, or you will get off.'

Cuyler's voice took on a frosty note.

'And what do you consider a fair rental to be?'

Pico Rodriquez pursed his lips.

'Shall we say two hundred dollars a month, dating from the time you first moved in?'

'We shall not!' rapped Cuyler harshly. He put his elbows on the table, leaned his big shoulders forward. 'Look, mister! You're on thin ice if you think you're going to hold me up. I never saw you before. I wonder if anybody else in Capell ever saw you before? You say you own that property. Well, maybe you do and maybe you don't. I'll have to see a lot more proof than just your casual word. Even if you do own it, you're not going to push me around. I'm fed right up to here—with being pushed around.'

Cuyler whipped a taut finger across his throat.

'You will pay me just rental or you will get off,' asserted Rodriquez again. 'The law will see to that.'

Cuyler's grin was bleak and mirthless. 'The words have a familiar ring. I've heard them from other lips. We'll see. Now, here comes my breakfast. If you don't mind—I want to enjoy it.'

Rodriquez pushed back his chair and stood up. His lips were thin and down curved.

'You'll hear from me again,' he purred. He paused at the counter to pay for his meal, then went out.

Cuyler rolled the thing over in his mind as he ate. It was pat. It was too pat. Cuyler remembered another man with dark skin and black, veiled eyes. Pierce Pomeroy, the banker. Behind this thing could be Pomeroy's hidden but treacherous touch. The thing to do, Cuyler decided, was wait the game out, for the moment, and watch developments.

On his way down to the corrals, Cuyler saw Paula Juilliard step out to the edge of the hotel porch, where the morning sun could strike her. She looked a little weary, but was smiling, as she looked down at Cuyler.

'Steve's doing nicely,' she reported. 'The first night is always the worst in a case like this, so Doctor Padgett says. I think we can be real optimistic, Gene.'

'You always make my world an easier one,' said Cuyler.

227

Her smile took on the old, tender, mysterious light. She yawned daintily, tapping her lips with the back of her hand.

'I've been on duty since midnight. I just came out for a moment in the sun before getting a little rest. I'll sleep better for having seen the old cast to your head and swing to your shoulders. I think, Gene, that the worst of the shadows are gone—for both of us.'

Cuyler worshipped her with his eyes.

'It will always be a brave world with people like you in it, Paula.'

Her eyes went very gentle. 'That is the nicest thing I ever had said to me. Say it to me again, sometime.'

She touched her fingertips to her lips, blew across them at him, then went back into the hotel.

Cuyler stood quietly for a moment, then went on his way.

Over at a window of the bank, Pierce Pomeroy stood, watching. His lips were repressed almost to nothingness and his eyes blind and black with hate.

* * *

Deputy U.S. Marshal Cade Booker was a short, thickset man with a blunt jaw and steel-gray eyes. As he stepped down from the dusty stage, Gene Cuyler was there to meet him. They shook hands. Booker looked around.

'Seems a nice quiet little town, Gene. But there must be trouble cooking or you wouldn't have sent for me.'

'The biggest chunk of trouble took place a week ago,' explained Cuyler. 'But your job is still ahead of you, Cade. Man, I'm glad to see you. You'll want the picture. Shall we eat while I explain?'

They spent a full hour in the Elite, Cuyler talking, Booker listening and eating between times.

'You feel sure that this Hitch Gower character shot that teamster of yours off his wagon, but that this banker was the guiding force behind it all, is that it?' remarked Booker.

'I can't see it any other way,' nodded Cuyler. 'I've laid out the whole line of reasoning and gone over it a hundred times in my mind. And everything checks. Hack Dowd was killed at a spot where, with his wagon running wild, it was sure to go off the grade into the canyon. It would take a man who had skinned a freight outfit across the Brushies to know such an exact spot. Hitch Gower was an ex-skinner, who knew every inch of the road between Capell and Sycamore. And the day I had cause to fire Gower for drunkenness and general orneriness, Pomeroy was there to see it. He heard Gower make the threat to get even with me.'

'And later, after the crime had been committed, you saw Pomeroy visit this Gower

229

at Gower's cabin, lay the law down to him then fork over five hundred dollars?' mused Booker, his keen eyes narrowed with thought.

'That's right, Cade. I think that was a payoff to get Gower to leave this part of the country and that Gower was on his way when I grabbed him.'

'There's a weak spot in your reasoning, Gene,' said the deputy marshal slowly. 'Two weak spots, in fact. If Pomeroy wanted you out of the picture, why didn't he turn this Gower hombre loose on your trail to dry-gulch you? And why should he have wanted to destroy a freight outfit he'd loaned you money to buy?'

'Those angles had me stumped for a time,' Cuyler admitted. 'But I think I finally came up with the right answers. In the first place, Pomeroy didn't want me put out of the picture at that time. Remember, the fight with the hostile cattle interests was still on then, and Pomeroy needed me to make the fight. At the same time, his strong card was to get me in debt to him to such an extent I couldn't possibly pay up when he decided the time was ripe to call my note. Hack Dowd and the outfit he was skinning, was bringing me in revenue and would continue to do so—while it rolled. But if it was washed out, then the loss was bigger to me than it was to him, and it shut off that revenue. You want to remember, Cade, Pomeroy had loaned me money to buy up five single-wagon outfits. But to get the loan I had

230

to put up not only five single outfits for collateral, but my other six double-wagon outfits as well. And he stood to grab the whole works, once he had me maneuvered into a corner.'

Booker nodded. 'I see—I see. The killing of the skinner, Dowd, was just incidental. It might have been any of your other skinners on that particular day. The first outfit that came along was the one to be sent over the grade and it was Dowd's hard luck that he happened to be driving it.'

'Right! You see, Cade, the reason I came to Capell in the first place was because, as I saw the setup, there was a real chance of building up a mighty profitable and long-term freighting business. I knew there was a fight ahead with the cattle interests, but it wouldn't be a lone fight. The wheat farmers would back my hand the same as I would back theirs, for I needed them and they needed me. I figured the combination would be strong enough to win that fight. It was. From here on in, wheat will go off these plains in ever-increasing quantities, and I'll be the man who hauls most of it.

'Now then, if I could figure that out, so could Pomeroy. He's a plenty shrewd hombre in money matters. And he figured to let me make the fight and win it. Then he'd step in, call a note I couldn't produce the ready cash for, take over my outfits and be all set up in the freighting business.'

Cade Booker nodded again, more emphatically. 'I get it. Even if you'd lost your fight, or got rocked off in it, Pomeroy still stood to come out ahead of the game. He could have sold your outfits for a lot more than he loaned against them. It was a case game. He couldn't lose, no matter what happened. But didn't he show his hand a little early? I wonder why?'

Gene colored slightly. 'Some personal angles that he hadn't considered at first were beginning to enter the picture. That was one thing. Then the big fire in the wheat fields and the burning of my hay might have scared him. On top of that, Hitch Gower, even though he'd been able to leave the country, would always have a club to wave over Pomeroy's head. A number of things to have made Pomeroy jittery.'

'But mainly—the personal angle,' observed Booker shrewdly. 'Could it—ah—perhaps be a lady?'

'A lady,' admitted Cuyler quietly. 'I'll see that you meet her, later. Right now we've things to do.'

'We have,' said Booker, getting to his feet. 'I want to have a talk with this fellow, Hitch Gower. And if the trail leads where we think it does, Mister Pierce Pomeroy will be next. Let's get about it.'

They headed down to the wagon camp and

saw Mike Kenna engaged in a heated argument with a swarthy, thin-faced individual. Mister Pico Rodriquez.

Cuyler jerked a nod.

'Another headache for me to figure out, Cade. That jigger yonder. Pico Rodriquez, he calls himself. Claims he owns this property where the corrals and the rest of the layout stands. Says it came down to him from his great-grandfather. He's trying to hold me up for a lot of rent, past and present and future. If I don't come through he aims to run me off.'

Booker's keen eyes sharpened, as he studied Rodriquez. Then he snorted.

'I'll cure that headache quick, Gene. Come on!'

Cade Booker went over to Kenna and the swarthy stranger. His voice bit coldly.

'Hello, Pasquale. When did you change your name to Rodriquez?'

The pseudo-Pico Rodriquez started, his black eyes flickering as he stared at the deputy marshal.

'You mistake me for another,' he said. 'My name is Pico—'

'Your name is Miguel Pasquale,' cut in Cade Booker bluntly. 'I, personally, gave you a floater out of Dyerville some two years ago as an undesirable tinhorn. Now you turn up here, still a tinhorn and still just as undesirable. Your kind does get around!'

The shiftiness in the beady eyes increased. 'I

233

tell you—'

Cade Booker cut in again. 'You're not telling me anything. You know I'm right. Just what's the play, anyhow?'

Gene Cuyler tried a shot in the dark.

'That's a good question. Here's another. How much did Pierce Pomeroy offer you to pull this little gag?'

Miguel Pasquale, of late, Pico Rodriquez, shrugged, admitting the game was up. A somewhat mealy smile loosened and mongrelized his lips completely.

'A man must make a living,' he smirked. 'And two hundred and fifty dollars is—two hundred and fifty dollars.'

'Once a tinhorn, always a tinhorn,' growled Cade Booker. 'But we may be able to use this little chunk of evidence, later. I suggest you hang on to him, Gene.'

'Right!' said Cuyler. 'Your chore, Mike. Keep him safe and out of sight.'

Mike Kenna locked a brawny hand on Pasquale's shoulder.

'So now it's me who'll be tellin' you, me fine bucko,' rumbled Mike, his brogue rich and burring. 'No shenanigans now, or it's a sorry one you'll be. Have no fears, Gene. He'll be right here when you want him.'

In saddle and on their way to Jim Nickerson's place, Cade Booker said, 'A man in my trade finds 'em in the queerest places.'

Gene Cuyler nodded.

234

'Another old friend of yours was around here, Cade. Gatt Ivance. Remember him in that timber trouble up at Burney? I figure he was the one who brought that phosphorus trick down here to burn wheat fields.'

'Of course I remember him,' said Booker. 'Is he still around?'

'Don't know. He wasn't a casualty the day of the big showdown fight. I'd feel better if he had been.'

'I noticed that gun under your jumper,' Booker observed. 'That why?'

'That's why. Gatt Ivance ran, up at Burney. Maybe this time he won't.'

'Smart,' said Booker. 'Don't get too contented until you have him located, Gene. You never can figure the breed of men like Gatt Ivance.'

They met Jim Nickerson at the ranch and Nickerson took them out to the seed wheat storeroom.

'This is one badly scared jigger I've kept locked up for you, Gene,' said Nickerson. 'He's sure got something on his mind.'

The rancher unlocked the storeroom door and they went in. Hitch Gower looked even worse than Cuyler figured he would. The ex-skinner was just a ghost of his former burly, swaggering self. Flesh had fallen away from him and his face had sagged into folds. His eyes were bloodshot, pouched and hunted. His heavy mouth was loose, his jaw pendulous. At sight of Cade Booker's badge, Gower cringed as though struck a blow.

'All right, Gene,' said Booker. 'Let me and this fellow have it out alone.'

Gene and Nickerson went out and closed the door. The rancher said, 'Whether or not you figured the results that way, Gene, the smartest thing you ever did was lock Gower up in that storeroom. Nothing to look at, nobody to talk to—I gave my cook who took over the chore of feeding him, orders that way. So all Gower could do was think and wonder and remember. He had no idea of what we knew for sure or what we didn't. All he could do was worry. Treatment like that would break a stronger man than Gower could ever hope to be. I think your friend Booker will come out with several answers.'

This was harvesting time. The plains were blanketed with a steady, ripe warmth. Out in Nickerson's biggest wheat field the McCormick harvester was rumbling and whirring, moving through a thin haze of dust and drifting chaff. Elsewhere the air was clear, the sky unmarred. The strip along the road lay black and charred, but the smoke of fire and men's hate was gone. A big farm wagon came rolling into the barns; loaded with sacked wheat which the harvester was dropping.

'I'm not forgetting that I was lucky,' said Nickerson. 'I'm splitting my crop with Abe Pettibone and Alec McKibbin, which will

236

carry everybody through for a fresh start next season.'

'That's damned white of you, Jim,' Cuyler observed.

Nickerson shrugged. 'It was everybody's fight. Why should it be one man's gain?'

A quarter of an hour later, Cade Booker came out of the storeroom. He spat, as though to clear his mouth of a foul taste. His voice was brittle with disgust.

'They're all alike, the men who do the dirty, mean, treacherous things in this life. In a pinch they fold and begin to whine. I never promised Gower a thing, but he gave me the whole story. Your theory and reasoning were exactly sound, Gene. Now for a talk with Mister Pierce Pomeroy.'

'And to think,' said Cuyler harshly, 'that I once heard Pomeroy philosophize on the nobility of some men and the baseness of others. The perfect hypocrite, Cade.'

Back in town Cade Booker headed for the bank, saying, 'I'll see you at the hotel in about an hour, Gene.'

Cuyler put up the horses, made sure Mike Kenna still had the imposter, Pasquale.

'The road ahead is clearing, Mike,' he said. 'We'll soon be rolling our wagons again and we'll do it in peace and with our guns left behind. It's a peace we've paid quite a price for.'

''Tis the way of the world, lad,' Mike

nodded. 'Some good things come free. The rest a man has to fight for.'

Cuyler went up town and turned in at the hotel, going into Steve Sears' room. Sam Reeves was there, chinning with Steve, who, propped up on pillows, was thin and gaunt but bright of eye. Cuyler grinned down at Steve.

'You're a tough young whelp. Sittin' up already. I expect he figures he'll he able to handle a jerkline again in a day or two, eh Sam?'

'I dunno about that,' answered the hotelkeeper, 'but he tells me I'm soon to lose him for a customer. Seems Candy Loftus has it figgered that a stay out at the J L headquarters will fix him up in fine shape. And Doc Padgett says they can move him out there the first of next week.'

'That right?' asked Cuyler of Steve.

Steve's old, boyish grin was back and working. 'Right—and I can't wait.'

'Huh!' grunted Cuyler. 'I suppose that means you'll stall off gettin' well just as long as you can, eh? Aiming just to lay around and make eyes at a pretty girl. Well, don't forget, my fine young friend, there's a wagon waiting for you to roll.'

Steve was hugely content. 'I ain't forgettin' a thing. But don't rush me. Bet you wish you were in my boots, yourself.'

'I'm satisfied with things just as they are,' said Cuyler. 'But you sure scared hell out of me for a while. Teach him to play chess, Sam. That'll keep him contented.'

Cuyler went down to the hotel porch, pulled up a chair and smoked some time away, waiting for Cade Booker. Cuyler's glance touched the front of the bank, and he wondered what was going on inside. In facing up to Pierce Pomeroy, Cade Booker was tangling with a different sort of customer than Hitch Gower had been. Pomeroy was shrewd, slick and not easily bluffed. But Cuyler also knew that Booker could be as tough as necessary. If anybody could force Pierce Pomeroy into a corner, Cade Booker was the man.

A buckboard rolled in at the upper end of the street. Driving was Ben Loftus. With him were Candy and Paula Juilliard. They pulled in at Gil Saltmarsh's store. Cuyler's glance fixed on Paula's dark head, shining in the sun.

The moment the buckboard stopped, Candy Loftus hopped lithely out, lifted a cloth-covered basket from the rear bed of the rig and came along the street toward the hotel.

Cuyler smiled to himself. Candy the reckless and headstrong, was bringing some sort of tasty food for Steve Sears. Those two kids—! There was no mistake the way the wind was blowing for them. Which made Steve's future something to think about. Maybe a partnership in the freighting setup. It was, Cuyler decided, an angle he'd put up to Steve,

239

later on. The promise of the future was big enough to justify it.

Cuyler left his chair, started up the street for the store. He grinned as he met up with the hurrying, eager Candy.

'Pie and cake and everything, I bet,' he teased. 'You watch out or you'll founder him, young 'un.'

Candy tossed her head with the old, well-remembered gesture. But her eyes were shining, her lips parted and softly smiling.

'It's only what Doctor Padgett said he could have. And Gene, Steve's to come out and stay at the ranch until he's well again.'

'So he was just telling me. Don't you baby him too much or he never will be tough enough again to handle a jerkline.'

Candy scurried along.

Cade Booker came out of the bank, lifted a hand to beckon Cuyler up. Cuyler started that way, and it was because he had fixed his glance on Booker that it took a vital moment before a softly shuffling movement at the mouth of the alley across the street, fully registered on his consciousness. Then it was like a bell, clashing softly in his brain. Cuyler whirled.

Gatt Ivance! There he stood in the alley mouth, a gun in each hand!

CHAPTER TWELVE

FINAL RECKONING

Gatt Ivance! Thin and malignant and gangling, those high shoulders, unmistakable anywhere, hunched forward. His words came across at Cuyler, tight and bitter, rising in a killing fury.

'You had a big hand in blocking me and running me out of Burney. You've had the whole hand in blocking me on those plains. You've been in my way too long, Cuyler—too damn long! When I ride on this time, I'll know you'll never show in my trail again. I'm through running from you. While you're through—all around!'

The round, blued steel muzzles of Ivance's guns were like the eyes of a snake, poised to strike. Ivance had the complete drop and there wasn't a thing, it seemed, that Cuyler could do. Ivance hadn't planned for any even break. He wasn't that sort. Ivance was out to kill, quickly and surely. Cuyler saw the final blaze of venom flood the gunman's eyes.

Sometimes, in the tightest corner of his life, a man was able to grasp a single lightning thought and act by it. At other times, sheer instinct guided him. It was so with Gene Cuyler, now. He dropped full length on his left side into the white dust of the street, his right hand darting under the left flap of his jumper. And the blast of Gatt Ivance's guns rolled at him.

It might have been the set certainty in Ivance's brain that he had Gene Cuyler dead to rights and so, having fixed the image of his target so definitely, he was unable instantly to change the pointing angle of his guns. Or it could have been that sheer chance alone had timed Cuyler's abrupt dropping out of line, timed it so finely that only fate could have calculated such split-second and inscrutable results. At any rate, Gatt Ivance missed, shooting where the broad target of Gene Cuyler's chest had been, but was not now.

The shock of his hitting the ground, seemed to drive the butt of Cuyler's gun into his hand. Then the weapon was out and stabbing at Ivance, the movement ending in pale flame and pounding report, beyond which the bitter cursing of Ivance was a thin and vicious echo.

Cuyler shot again—shot a third time. The muzzle blast of the heavy revolver, driving out from so close to the ground, kicked dust from the street and sent it whirling, making of Cuyler's target only a thin and bending shadow, through a sifting gray shroud. Cuyler threw a fourth shot through that whipping dust.

All the time Cuyler was tensed, waiting the shock of driving lead. A bullet struck over him,

242

whimpering away in buzzing flight. Another struck just short of him, showering him with dust. Though Cuyler did not know it, at that exact moment, these were the final desperate tries of a man virtually dead on his feet. Having got them off, blind and hopeless, Gatt Ivance took two uncertain steps forward and lunged out on his face. He lay, sprawled and limp, his head hanging over the edge of the board sidewalk. Gene Cuyler's second shot had done this, tearing through Ivance's chest, heart-high.

Cuyler climbed up out of the dust, dazed and almost numb with disbelief.

Cade Booker came racing up, to catch at Cuyler.

'Gene! Where'd he hit you, man?'

Cuyler shook himself, swung his head slow negation. His answer was a mecha mumble.

'He didn't. He never touched me. He dead to rights—and he never touched

Down from the store came anothe figure, slim, dark-haired, half sobl ran.

'Gene! Oh, my dear—my dear

Then Paula Juilliard's arm mad Cuyler, clinging to him, while again. name again and again. Cuyler of curious into the fragrance of her world steadied and grew s

Cade Booker directed

men with swift, brusk efficiency. The lank, loose figure of Gatt Ivance, who had reached the end of every gunman's trail, was carried quickly away. That done, Booker turned and looked at those two standing there in the street, still lost to everything except each other.

His keen eyes softened and his words were a murmur for his own ears.

'Down along the trail I've seen the percentage work, and sometimes it comes out right. A man might guess the value of a card in the center of a fresh deck and marvel at the ᵈds if he guesses right. But who cares about ᵃs long as the called card turns up? I had ᵗo believe that Gatt Ivance could have ᵗhat distance.'

shadowed window of the bank, y laid the hard blackness of his ₑe street. He saw the hurrying ₑm mass and move away, ₗance. He saw Gene Cuyler and heᵢcked in each other's arms and the ᵦd the blood behind his eyes Theₕhing in a crimson haze. And broughtᵣ, now moving back toward

aᵃ hand under his coat, nosed, nickel-plated gun. ₜ was a long shot out to would have to move to ᵗhₒot. And there would be y-eyed man of the law,

in
nical
had me

The
brought
For such
Gene Cuyle
the door to try
Cade Booker, th

4

to block his way.

From the very first, it seemed, something had always appeared to block his way to Gene Cuyler. Despite the deep-laid cunning of his plans, unguessed and unforeseen factors had cropped up to thwart him.

The things this Cade Booker had told him, in such hard and unrelenting words. Hitch Gower, broken and cowering, telling all about the killing of Hack Dowd. The unmasking of Pasquale, the impostor, and the story he had to tell. The use of these two hirelings had seemed such good strategy at the time. But Pomeroy realized now that both had been mistakes. Gower—he should have taken steps while he had the chance, should have silenced Gower for good, once he had used him.

Something began to grow inside of Pierce Pomeroy, a cold and shaking conviction of utter impotency and helplessness. He knew that the law had him. At the worst that law would hang him. At the best it would put him behind bars for long years, maybe all of the years left to him. And that could be the worst of all.

Where and when had the first break come in the carefully planned fabric of his life? What had been the first mistake? Why had he fumbled—?

Something was closing about him, a gray and icy shroud. He looked again at the gun he held. The bank teller, a little, mousy man, who had been watching Pomeroy anxiously, called in thin alarm.

'Mister Pomeroy—!'

Pierce Pomeroy did not hear him. He could hear nothing now but the steps of Cade Booker, coming closer, almost to the door. The step of the law coming for him, ominous and remorselessly certain.

The sound became more than the stride of a single man. It became the thunderous, beating roll of a whole world of men, advancing on him through the written law which they had devised for the good of all. And he was the transgressor—!

Something snapped in Pierce Pomeroy's brain. Here was the final checkmate!

He put the nickel-plated gun to his head and pulled the trigger. . . .

*　　　*　　　*

They sat on the porch of the J L ranchhouse. The first soft dusk was flowing over the land in a tide of peace. Paula Juilliard reached a slim hand across the arm of her chair and Gene Cuyler took it gently in both of his.

Ben Loftus came out of the house, glanced at the two of them. He spoke with a mock grumbling which did not hide his huge content.

'I don't rate nothin' around this house any more. Inside I see Candy and that young cub of a Steve holdin' hands, and their eyes so full of

246

stars they can't even notice me. I come out here and you two are just as bad. I suppose I'll have to spend my evenin's in the bunkhouse from now on, playin' two-bit stud with the saddle hands.'

Paula Juilliard laughed softly. 'First thing you know, Uncle Ben, you'll be growing old and crochety.'

Ben Loftus grunted and pounded his pipe on the porch rail.

Gene Cuyler said, 'I got a letter from Cade Booker today, Ben. After turning Hitch Gower over to the proper authorities, Cade spent some time looking up some old records in the land office. He found an item that showed that a certain Don Tomás Rodriquez ceded two square miles of his old rancho to the township of Capell. Which means that the property that's been used for corrals and a wagon camp, is town and public property. So I'll have no more trouble on that angle.'

'That's fine,' growled Loftus. 'Trouble! I never want to hear of such again. But that's life, I reckon. It takes a wild ride over a rough trail to make a man appreciate smooth goin'. Well, that poker game should be under way by this time. Let me know how many stars there are when you get through countin' 'em.'

Loftus went over to the bunkhouse.

Paula Juilliard gripped Gene Cuyler's hand with sudden fierceness. Cuyler, understanding, patted her hand softly.

'Forget it, girl—it's all over with now.'

'I try,' she said. 'But every now and then it comes back to me so strongly. The rumble of the guns and sight of you, lying in the street. I just quit living right then, Gene—until I saw you get up and knew that you were all right...'

She bit at soft, red lips and her eyes filled. Cuyler spoke quietly.

'Life always calls for a lot of forgetting. But now we can begin living things worth remembering. For all of a lifetime.'

Her eyes cleared and the old, tender, mysterious smile softened her lips.

'For all of a lifetime,' she murmured softly.

The night held them still, dreaming. This still and resting world that held their future. Daylight and dark. Earth, sky, sunshine and rain. Grazing cattle. Golden wheat fields, nodding in the sun. The sweet winds of space.

And the open road, open for all time, now. With the yoke bells clashing and singing, and the dusty wagons rolling—

Matt Stuart was the byline used by L. P. Holmes on a number of outstanding Western novels. Born in a snowed-in log cabin in the heart of the Rockies near Breckenridge Colorado in 1895, Holmes moved with his family when very young to northern California and it was here that his father and older brothers built the ranch house where Holmes grew up and where, in later life, he would live again. He published his first story—'The Passing of the Ghost'—in *Action Stories* (9/25). He was paid ½¢ a word and received a check for $40. 'Yeah—forty bucks,' he said later. 'Don't laugh. In those far-off days ... a pair of young parents with a three-year-old son could buy a lot of groceries on forty bucks.' He went on to contribute nearly 600 stories of varying lengths to the magazine market as well as to write over fifty Western novels under his own name and Matt Stuart. For the many years of his life, Holmes would write in the mornings and spend his afternoons calling on a group of friends in town, among them the blind Western author Charles H. Snow whom Lew Holmes always called 'Judge' Snow (because he was Napa's Justice of the Peace 1920–1924) and who frequently makes an appearance in later novels as a local justice in Holmes's imaginary Western communities. Holmes's Golden Age as an author was from 1948 through 1960. During these years under his Matt Stuart byline he produced such notable novels as

Dusty Wagons, *Gunlaw at Vermillion*, *Wire in the Wind*, *Sunset Rider*, and *Gun Smoke Showdown*. This last was reprinted in paperback under the title *Saddle-Man*. In these novels one finds the themes so basic to his Western fiction: the loyalty which unites ones man to another, the pride one must take in his work and a job well done, the innate generosity of most of the people who live in Holmes's ambient Western communities, and the vital relationship between a man and a woman in making a better life.

We hope you have enjoyed this Large Print book. Other Chivers Press or G.K. Hall Large Print books are available at your library or directly from the publishers. For more information about current and forthcoming titles, please call or write, without obligation, to:

Chivers Press Limited
Windsor Bridge Road
Bath BA2 3AX
England
Tel. (01225) 335336

OR

G.K. Hall
P.O. Box 159
Thorndike, ME 04986
USA
Tel. (800) 223–6121
(207) 948–2962
(in Maine and Canada, call collect)

All our Large Print titles are designed for easy reading, and all our books are made to last.